D0912193

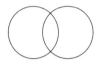

Venus&Document

a novel

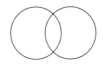

Jared Marcel Pollen

CROWSNEST BOOKS

Crowsnest Books
www.crowsnestbooks.com

Distributed by the University of Toronto Press

ISBN: 9780921332862 (paperback)

ISBN: 9780921332879 (ebook)

Cataloguing Information available from Library and Archives Canada

Printed and bound in Canada

"What is happening everywhere is, one way or another, known to everyone. Shadowy world tides wash human nerve endings in the remotest corners of the earth."

– Saul Bellow, "There is Simply Too Much to Think About"

"Supposing that Truth is a woman—what then?"

– Nietzsche, *Beyond Good & Evil*

Prologue

I find myself oddly contemplative in times of crisis. More contemplative than usual, that is. After all, crises encourage us to see ourselves as participants in the great cultural drama, players living through hinge moments in history, and with this comes the heavy business of worldly reflection. These days, "crisis" is an ongoing phenomenon, which means that our perspective must constantly refresh itself. The German philosopher Hegel said that the owl of Minerva takes flight only with the gathering of dusk, meaning that an epoch is only understood after the fact; we can't really know what we've experienced until it's passed. True, certainly. But who has the time for that?

It was 8:15 and I was writing the first draft of history. The shades of dusk had gathered over New York, and we were living through what was already being deemed a catastrophe, or that most abused media-term, a tragedy. A macro-storm, a nor'easter, had descended on the city the previous evening, shutting down sections of its electrical grid and reducing the borough's lower levels to submarine darkness. It was another Sandy-type event, another one of the biblical disasters that seemed to strike this side of the American coastline every annum. Last year it had been Puerto Rico, the year before that, Texas. And although I was safely ensconced in a restaurant on the Upper

West Side, in my mind, my fingers were already queuing up over the keys.

Karen Marlowe, perhaps sensing this inward course of thought, asked the acutely feminine question:

"What are you thinking?"

I was looking at photos of the storm on my phone. There was one in particular, a looming aerial perspective, acquired the night before by some cloud-scraping chopper: Manhattan Island, its bottom darkly reconfigured, arteries of light trimming the east and westside highways, buildings dimly gleaming on backup generators, the southern embankments blown over with spume, access roads transformed into quick canals, the bridges over the East River flickering and going dead at their centers.

"Nothing," I said.

We sat at a corner booth in low light, under girderwork hung with Edison bulbs, their coils burning noiseless. I felt slightly above my station, being here with affluent Manhattanites, all vastly more important than myself. But I wasn't about to protest. Karen Marlowe was a beautiful shamble of a woman, a photographer and a cosmopolitan breed who embraced the transient pleasures of an unquiet life. We had a professional respect for one other, and there was little to our relationship beyond the fact that we happened to work for the same magazine. She was, like so many people in my life, a contact, a name in a list.

"Nothing," I said. "Stop kicking me."

"You've got something. I can see it."

"Don't worry about it, okay."

"Well don't look so morose."

"What morose? I'm sitting here."

"You've got that hundred-mile stare. Absent, brooding."

"I'm thinking," I said.

"So am I. But I don't look like that."

I checked my phone again. I noticed others around me doing the same, their faces caged in LED light. I pulled down and refreshed the page, amazed by the sheer number of updates that had occurred in only a few minutes. They were showing footage of flooded areas all over the city: floating neighborhoods in Queens, Westchester, and Brooklyn, homeowners venturing out to remove items from their cars, bearing possessions above their heads, garden tables being carried out to the river, loading docks and airport runways vanished under a greengray undescribed surface.

The screen went to sleep and I caught sight of myself, mirrored in the gorilla glass. I was pale, in need of sleep. Karen too looked lagged and bloodshot. She'd just gotten in after a nineteen-hour flight and her mind was still in another time zone.

"I have to write a piece about the storm and submit it tomorrow morning," I said.

"What if we do something together?" It took me a moment to catch the meaning. "Would Bill object if you submitted the article with images?"

"You want to go out in this?"

"Sure, why not?" she said. "We'll walk downtown and see what we can get."

· 4 ·

"I don't know if this is the time to go running around outside."

"When everybody else is running inside, I'm running outside. I was in Dubai last month when a sandstorm broke. Those things are brutal. They were telling everyone in the hotel to stay away from the windows and take cover while I was trying to convince the manager to let me onto the roof."

"I wish I had your courage."

"Still, it leaves one longing for the inside life. The comfort of a desk."

"I have a good view from my workspace," I said, "so I feel I always have one foot outside. When I first moved to the city, I used to write with the windows open—even in the winter— just to feel nearer to it all. I still do, sometimes. When I get lonely, I open the windows and the city consoles me."

Because of her job Karen never stayed in the city long enough to have a proper home. She had a small flat in Dumbo (a nook, a closet) which was currently under water, so she asked if she could stay with me for the next few evenings.

"It'll be nice to go out and walk around. I've been on the road so long I feel like a stranger in my own town," she said, sectioning off a piece of meat. "Whenever I see this city now it's always from the window of a fuselage, or an office in the middle of a skyscraper. I stand next to people in elevators and I can't imagine a single thing about their lives. You know that three of my friends have had kids while I've been away—and I haven't met any of them? And every time I come home it seems like there's a new skyline. I feel like I've missed a million things."

Karen was like an astronaut back from a year in low-orbit, fresh out of a vacuum and eager to hear the stories of earthlings. Her eyes hovered above her glass, examining me. They were red-dark, like cherrywood, their black grain bleeding through.

"Tell me about your life, Paul. I'm desperate."

"What's to tell? I'm single, underpaid, and overeducated. I took a year off from the college. Not a wise decision, financially, but I needed the time. Call it paid leave for higher thought. I have an idea for a big thing, but I don't know what it is yet."

The restaurant was nearly full, packed with foodies in a festive mood. I'd expected the city to suspend its activities in light of the storm, slow down, spend a few nights in the dark. But up here, on the unflooded half of the island, people were going about living. It seemed to be both the day of and the day after. The storm also brought out a sense of whimsy and abandon, the kind you got when the order of things was disturbed. On social media people were using the last of their battery life to post photos of themselves reading by candlelight, embracing this temporary suspension of normality. And here in the restaurant, they carried on like kids on a snow day, their conversations buzzing over brown cocktails. All eyes were on the city and we felt like participants in some global event.

It was hard not to feel this way. Yesterday afternoon I'd picked up Karen on one of the last flights into LaGuardia before they closed down the sky. She'd been in the streets of Tokyo a day earlier. Japanese still rang in her ears. And now here we were, dining somewhere on the Upper West Side:

our steaks from upstate, our wine from Italy, our wine glasses from Mexico, the waiter Welsh, the furniture Danish modern, our phones designed in California and made in China with Coltan metal from the Congo; and this was to say nothing of my thoughts, which had been browsing a bunch of cultures (Greeks, Germans, ancients, and moderns) all day long. And yet the restaurant seemed visibly invested in bucking the forces of globalism (everything was advertised as "locally sourced" and "home-grown"). This was, in effect, a petty-bourgeois statement against neoliberalism and its discontents, and it seemed to make people feel good about themselves. So it was, you couldn't even order a steak in this city without making some kind of statement about late capitalism.

I swiped through webpages of satellite imagery, interactive maps, Doppler radars showing rainbow spirals, nebulous masses churning. I found a map of the city that showed the boroughs trimmed blue along their edges and marked "Disaster Areas." Then the trim switched to green and expanded, blotting out more of the land. A chart appeared and this time it read, "Flood Levels." Then it switched once more to orange and read "Category Four." I watched a video of an anchor walking around a huge lit floor in the center of some Midtown studio. He was using a remote to manipulate a computer-generated model that rose up around his feet. He crouched down as the model grew and rotated to an aerial view, so that he now stood directly on top of the streets. He began pointing out spots where the power had gone out, as a digital tide rose around his shoes.

"We'll have to walk," I said. "No taxis will take us downtown."

Now shots of ConEd men in Day-Glo gear, knee-deep in water, the mouth of a subway station churning foam, frothing at the steps, choking the drains; shuttered storefronts and dead streetlights swinging, a lot of yellow cabs reduced to their roofs, abandoned construction sites with collapsed perimeter fences and tarps smacking in the wind.

When I looked up, Karen was staring at me.

"Join us, will you?"

Another detail about Karen: she had a birthmark near the back of her left cheek the color of a wine stain and shaped like a bowling pin, and when she drew her black hair back with the comb she made of her hand (like she was doing now) it stuck out like the moon in a starless sky.

She told me stories as we walked through Midtown, a light rain falling. The aggregate LED displays worked on overhead, lonely without their audience. Above a line of trees at Bryant Park, the Empire State loomed as a dim, geometric obscurity. Karen cradled her camera in her chest like a kitten.

I made her tell me about the dangerous missions, the trips into Central Africa and the Middle East, the kind of assignments that required combat boots and parachuting out of an airliner into enemy territory, the nights she spent squatting in the jungle, eating out of mess tins, urinating in a mosquito heat. These were the dramatic big-screen terms in which I conceived of her job. Photojournalism was an extreme sport, an adventurous enterprise like archeology, calling on equal measures of bravery and craft. Karen seemed to entertain this

· 8 ·

fantasy when she used words like *point* and *shoot* and *aim*, the language of heavy weaponry.

We passed a team of reporters—men shouldering cameras out of trunks, people with earpieces speaking in clipped and coded language. More ConEd men were gathered around the base of a fallen crane. Its collapsed frame ran nearly the length of the block, lying neatly between the parked cars. Because it didn't appear to have caused any real harm, I didn't feel guilty about finding the scene intriguing. In general, I hadn't thought of the storm as something truly menacing. I thought of it in the way Barthes had written about the floods in Paris in the fifties, as an antic moment of mythic splendor. I recalled those black-and-white photos of French men rowing boats down the rues and lily-hopping from chair to chair to cross the street.

We came to 34th street and went into darkness. Karen wandered off, looking up a cluster of buildings through her viewfinder. I took out my phone. Raindrops tapped the screen, making little rainbows. There was an article about a car bomb at an airport in Istanbul, but this seemed like lesser news now. The storm was the top story everywhere. It had risen above all others and made a claim on the world's attention. A recent viral video was also trending again. A few months ago, a teenage girl from Sweden had spoken at a climate summit in Paris, in which she tearfully castigated world leaders for their utter failure to address the catastrophe of climate change. It became one of the most watched videos online, with something like two billion viewers. Now people were posting it again in direct response to the storm.

Karen reappeared, camera slung across her chest like a bandolier. She rubbed her hands and used my sleeve to wipe off the lens. She used a Nikon F, the Kalashnikov of cameras. She hated digital and refused to use it. The whole point of the photograph is the imprinted moment, she said, the flash-capture, and the way you had to wait to find out what you'd seen.

We walked down a side street, between dark up-jutting perpendiculars. I saw people on fire escapes, drinking and laughing, their faces bottomlit by the glow of their devices. By now we had entered SoHo and the cobble streets were filled to the curbs. Karen removed her sneakers and went barefoot through the water with her pants cuffed. She told me a story about how she ate a bowl of bull eyeballs with Sherpas while tracking wild horses across the Gobi Desert, and how she smoked something strange and saw the sunrise in that place, which was the most beautiful thing you'd ever seen, but she didn't have any pictures because she'd run out of film, and now she could barely remember it.

Karen said she took photos to locate herself, to remind herself where she was and where she had been.

In about an hour we made it to the High Line, a block of raised-railway-cum-promenade. From the walkway we climbed a set of metal steps to the roof of the Whitney Museum. Around us, the shadowed tons hung in silence. Karen snapped away, pulling back the wind with her thumb and releasing it like a bolt-action rifle. I saw the work-in-progress of a new tower, its unfinished glass half still lit, the iron interior rising up and disappearing into darkness. Out in the bay, toward

Staten Island, the lights of distant industry marked out the spot where the earth met the sky.

Having spent the afternoon reviewing a book on the Romantics, I thought, as Wordsworth might have, of the sea that bares her bosom to the moon and the winds that will be howling at all hours, about how we wasted true opportunities for contemplation with all our "getting and spending"—and how nothing moves us anymore. The winds were howling, certainly, but perhaps we were moved too much now, in every possible direction. At the moment, a thousand different connections seemed available to me (the landscape practically shuttered with them) all ready to go with meaning, as easy to call upon as they were to discard.

Karen asked me to lean against the railing and look into the distance so that she could take a picture.

"Look like you're thinking about something important," she said.

When we got home, we found every door in the hallway open. People moved in and out of neighboring rooms, mingling with those from lower floors, exchanging stories, sharing coffee, suddenly friends. A young boy was riding his tricycle back and forth across the carpet while other kids played invented hallway games—"you're-it" and "first-one-to-the-elevator." These were the little connections, the shared moments waiting to be anecdotes in our future lives.

Karen dropped her bags in the foyer and walked to the kitchen without turning on the light. She rolled up her sleeves, an unconscious gesture, caught in a moment of paralyzed reflection, maybe the first real one in weeks.

"Whiskey," she said.

I filled a glass and went about the apartment with the bottle, leaving the lights off. I sprung the latch on the windows and looked out over the dark body of the park.

"This is cute," she said. "I mean, it's got that writerly vibe."

"It's above my pay grade," I said. "I like the idea of living on the West Side, but I can't afford it."

"I've been on the road for forty-three weeks. I don't want to move more than fifteen feet for the next few days, alright?"

"You'll stay here," I said. "I'll make you dinner. In the evenings we'll watch movies."

She sorted through the drawers absently, not looking for anything.

"I'm going to finish this drink standing if you don't mind," she said. "I see that kitchen table and I realize I haven't sat at mine for almost a year and I'm kind of fucking terrified at the prospect, understand."

"I'll draw you a bath. You know, I've always loved that phrase—*draw* a bath. We don't use it for anything else, do we?"

"No, I need to sleep. God, I need to sleep,"

I went to the window and climbed onto the gated ledge, bracing myself against the lintel. Not much was happening, just the numbered awnings snapping in the breeze. The rain changed into mist, which didn't fall so much as cling to the air, and there was a bit of lightning in the distance, flashbulbs taking pictures inside the clouds. My phone vibrated in my pocket. It was a call from Jim Uppendahl, a man whose status in my life was constantly shifting between the friendly and the professional, the personal and the political. If he was calling me at this hour, it was because he wanted to exchange ideas.

"Do you know what time it is?" I said.

"We need to convene tomorrow," he said. "Serious discourse."

"I have to get some work done."

"What can you be working on?"

"It's the storm."

"You've always got something to say. What's one more article going to accomplish?"

"Writers build their credibility through quantity, Jim. It's about repetition and constant output. It's how we earn the public's trust. We can't all make one film and hit it big."

"Who was it that said you only ever write one book and then you spend the rest of your life writing different versions of that book?"

"Oh, I know this."

"And I've made two films."

Karen wandered the flat absently, scanning bookshelves in the dark.

"It's got to be before the dinner hour, though," he said. "Eleanor and I have obligatory Sunday outings now. Strengthen morale you know. A marriage crying out for structure."

"I've decided I can't."

"The first thing I learned when I met you is that you're a terrible liar, Paul"

"I'm guessing you won't be flying out for the film festival?"

"Tomorrow," he said, then hung up.

I climbed back inside and peeled off my socks. Karen stood at the shelf with a book open. I took it from her hands.

"I'll put our clothes in the dryer," I said.

She sat on the edge of the sofa as I helped her off with her pants, tugging them from each wet leg, which she raised lazily like a kid before bedtime.

"What time is it?" she said. "Wait, don't answer that."

She undressed and slipped off to bed. The book she'd pulled was a copy of Voltaire's selected works. I flipped to the poem he'd written about the 1755 Lisbon earthquake, in which he argued that if such a disaster was possible, then God—if he existed—was either a) not all powerful, or b) not all good. This proved to be a breakthrough in modern thought, a major blow to God, theodicy, and to the whole universe as we understood it. So what, I thought, could this disaster do for us? What new narratives would emerge? How would it change any of us, if at all? And if we had anyone like Voltaire in our time, would people care about what he had to say? Would he make the news cycle? Would they put him on CNN at 6:00 and sit him down next to the pundits and the climate scientists to discuss these things?

Soon, images from the night began calling themselves up in montage. I couldn't be sure which bits belonged to the things we'd seen or to the footage I'd watched. I wandered the dark apartment, trying to force the moment to some culmination—but it withheld itself. The message Nature seemed to be sending us was that some order had been disturbed; the world was in full revolt. And I was seized by the need to explain, to unpack things and put them in their place, to order what needed to be ordered ("The time is out of joint; O cursed spite!").

I checked my phone again. Social media was blowing up with people talking about the storm, discussing the present as if it were already the past. This commentary also seemed to be an important element in the event. It wasn't on top of it, over it, after it—it was part of it. This was the real phenomenon: not the flood, but that we were here to record it, remember it, share it at the speed of light. I pulled down on the page a few more times, watching the little throbber spin. I didn't even know what I was looking for anymore. I felt drained, disoriented. I got down and laid myself out in the middle of the floor. I stayed there for I don't know how long, starshaped, splayed, as raindrops rang on the iron bars of the escape and the city rolled on under night.

&

I came up from the tunnel into a hemorrhage of noise and light. The yellow metal of taxis clogged the street while pedestrians hustled through the jam. I merged with the stream and headed for the setback deco building with the sunburst doors and machine-age idols looking out over the balustrade. Kiosks lined the sidewalk, vendors selling high-resolution images of the landmarks that were all around us—if you were a tourist, the things you saw a thousand times before you actually saw them—images that lay somewhere between the folds of memory and representation.

For the last two years, I'd been working as a staff writer at a fairly prestigious but financially declining New York magazine, where I penned two pieces a month on literature, politics, or culture. I landed the job after I met Bill Morning, my future editor, at a launch party downtown. I'd already gotten a fair amount of attention for some essays I'd written for various websites and blogs, and Bill wanted to cultivate me as a new critical voice. The sense was that I was an up-and-coming thinker to be reckoned with, a voice that "couldn't be ignored" (in someone's formulation). I'd even developed something of an audience, or so I was told. I wasn't on social media at that point, uninterested in its vanity project of self-promotion and accumulating followers, which I considered to be beneath the work of a serious writer. But it became clear that I was behind on what was happening in the culture, and I was all but forced into creating profiles on several platforms, because that was just the way things were now, Bill said, you had to "be your own brand" and stuff, because social media—when it wasn't actively contributing to the death of journalism—could at least be used to prop up its remains. I'd accumulated a decent following since then (five figures, not bad by literary standards) but to date, hadn't managed to produce anything of real significance, the kind of thing that would overturn people's attention and "break the internet," as they say. Most of the time, my articles seemed to disappear almost as quickly as they went up. The pace of events was relentless, and whatever you published, no matter how poignant, how true, was irrelevant within days, or hours, disappearing in the endless scroll. The truth was publication meant very little. It was the anticipation of waiting for an article to go up—the sense of impending significance—that was everything.

I met Bill in the lobby and he took me down to the basement, where the magazine stored its old and disused presses. We walked through a draped factory space, under rows of lean fluorescent lights, along ranks of soundless dark machinery, passing presses and editing stations, tracks and cages and conveyor belts, a rack of pistons suspended mid-motion. It was as if we were touring the engine room of a massive ocean liner abandoned to the sea floor. Bill climbed an iron catwalk elevated above a sorting unit, looking out in a wide meditative state.

"Those were great nights," he said, addressing the room in an elegiac tone. "When a story would come in and we'd fire up these machines." He extended his finger to the far wall. "Those doors would open out onto the street and men would come and load bales of paper onto the trucks. I remember the smell of diesel exhaust and the sight of the trucks disappearing into the night, ready to deliver stories to a hungry public."

Bill was one of the old guard, the last of a dying kind who came up during the golden age of adversarial journalism in the 1970s, when public trust in institutions was at its lowest. He'd lived through the Pentagon Papers, Watergate, Iran-Contra, and still had elevated notions about what the news could do. Most of all, he understood the quasi-spiritual relationship people had with the media, how desperate the human need for "perspective," how crucial it was for our imagination and survival to know what you're living through and how things are in the world.

The light fell faintly on his head, his big silver face frozen in quarter-profile like a man on a dollar bill. He adhered to the modest one-outfit policy of CEOs and entrepreneurs: jeans, running shoes, black turtleneck, high-shoulders framed in a blazer. He was large, ambling, soft, bespectacled, liver spotted, his hair combed back into peppered waves.

"That was a damn fine piece you wrote on the storm," he said. "If they ever publish a collection of your work, make sure that one's in it."

"Thanks, Bill."

"How's Karen?"

"Oh, you know."

"Insane."

"Completely insane."

"You could send that woman into a minefield."

"Yeah, insane."

He came down the stairs, slow and heavy, his ring scraping against the rail.

"I'd ask you how Elsa is," I said.

"But small talk has never been your thing. Am I at least allowed to ask you what you're working on right now? It's one of my few obligations as an editor."

"It's your only obligation, Bill."

"Elsa's fine, by the way."

"These days, I get up and I can only think in loose phrases, snatches of things. I've been living in notes for weeks, piles of ideas I can't get out from under. I find myself seizing up halfway through a sentence, convinced there's a thousand other ways I could roll out this thought."

"Well, I won't probe you. I know better than that. Besides, this is a friendly visit."

"We've never had friendly visits, Bill."

He worked at the buttons on his cuffs as if to distract himself from some unpleasant thought settling back into his mind.

"I'm glad you came," he said. "I'll let you know now that the rumors of my leaving are entirely true."

"There were rumors?"

"The office is going to send out an email on Friday."

"I had no idea."

Advance Reader Copy

"My doctors recently made two discoveries: the first is a tumor the size of a dime in my esophagus, which—if I press here" he drew back his collar, "I can actually feel some days."

"Cancer?"

"They never say cancer. That's the thing. First they tell you to go see an oncologist. Then they tell you they want to start treatment in a few weeks. Chemotherapy and radiation. Then somewhere between the elevator and the parking lot you realize you're one of those people now."

"What are the odds?"

"They have numbers for these things, probability exercises. At this stage, a third of all people make it to a year, and beyond that, a fifth make it another three years, and so on. Your survival becomes a statistic. Anyway, they're not good. The numbers."

"What are your options?"

"My options are that I also have early onset Alzheimer's, which is all still very vague and far ahead. They can't say much with certainty right now. But apparently I'm a 'good candidate.'"

"Jesus Christ, Bill."

"Right now, the best-case scenario for the cancer is three years," he said, patting the back of his neck. "The Alzheimer's is due to kick in in about five-to-seven, they think. It'll start with me forgetting my keys; after that I'll be pissing in the sink and getting lost on my way to the mailbox."

"Fuck." I was unable to say anything else.

"It's one or the other. I'm not even out of my sixties and I've already been given two ways to die. If I beat one, the other will be waiting to take me down."

"So you're going to reject treatment?"

"And die with dignity? Yes."

"I always thought of you as the kind of guy who would be at the desk until he died," I said.

"I planned on it."

"Why not give yourself another five to ten years, if it's in the cards?"

"I don't want my illness to define me. If I have another ten years in me, I live them as a sick man. I don't want to be known as the sick man. So, me and Elsa are going to do everything we've always wanted to do but haven't had the time for."

"And you don't feel bad about jumping ship?"

"The life ship?"

"The journalism ship."

"I prefer to think of it as going down with it," he said. "The business has changed. Journalism used to have real rage and flare. You stayed up all night in the hotel fueled on whiskey to get those three-thousand words, then you flew home and went to a party with models and diplomats while your words moved off the shelves in the stores beneath you."

"That hasn't been my life."

"God, it was brilliant."

"Hold on Bill, I'm still trying to understand."

"Now people with cellphones get to the news first. A bomb goes off in Egypt and the video is shared a million times over before you can even finish your draft. And when you get your

Advance Reader Copy

article out there, there's a thousand others to choose from, a thousand different points of view. People don't know how to handle it. You talk to them on the street and they say, 'I don't even know what to think anymore.' And I'm one of them, Paul."

"If you're trying to get me worked up, you're succeeding," I said. "We're wallowing in overproduction. I was going on about this the other night with Karen."

We took the elevator up and maneuvered through a floor of screens, desks, and lamps. Bill's office was crowded with vegetation. He felt plants helped you think and he took oxygenation to the extreme. We sat with each other in the receding light of his twenty-fourth-floor office. He had the look of an aging and self-preserving ivy-leaguer, a Yale man, who still went to collegiate football games and got drunk with the boys once a summer in Martha's Vineyard. He'd managed to stay well connected beyond his profession, lunching with senators, justices, diplomats. He didn't need the news. If he wanted to know what was happening on Capitol Hill, he could call his friends.

He looked up, searching for something in the air above him.

"Have you given any thought to how you want to be processed, Paul?"

"Processed?"

"Buried, cremated, donated to science, dumped at sea?"

"I just turned thirty-three, Bill. Little early to be thinking about that."

"Jesus died at thirty-three."

"So did Alexander. So did a lot of people."

"Elsa's lived in constant fear of my death. She always said she wanted to go first because she just couldn't handle it. On vacation she would have visions of me collapsing in our hotel room. She'd talk about having to buy a coffin to fly my body back; how the baggage handlers would stuff me in the cargo with the luggage, somebody's golf clubs lying on top of me."

"Bill, I'm really trying to find something to say about this."

"At least I'll have a chance to read a few pre-emptive obituaries," he said. "Which is a privilege given to few."

He told me about how the magazine had a cache of obituaries prepared for certain notable people—ex-presidents, athletes, celebrities. In the event any of them died suddenly, the memorials would be ready to go within minutes.

"We commission at least a few pre-emptive obituaries every year," he said, "for people who we think are on the verge."

"Who's in there?"

"Oh, I'm sure it wouldn't surprise you."

I pictured a folder waiting in some hard drive somewhere, filled with documents named after those who had already been proclaimed dead, who had been written off and had their legacies decided in advance.

"And who's been writing them?" I said, "You didn't invite me here to write yours, did you?"

"Someone's already written mine, I'm sure."

"Read your own obituary, gives you a new lease on life."

"Who said that?"

"Leopold Bloom."

"Always quoting, Paul. I've got some scotch in the filing cabinet over here. Twelve-year. Business gift."

"I can't stay Bill, I'm sorry."

I checked my phone and made to get up. In the window the low evening light was dying across town, slipping between the buildingscape and settling into various lengths of amber and shadow. Bill dipped the brown bottle over a silver dish, filling two frosted glasses; the liquid chuckled through the slender neck.

"I was only half-telling-the-truth earlier when I said this was a friendly visit."

"So, you didn't invite me here just to tell me you were dying?"

"Have you heard about this demonstration in Paris?" he said.

"Vaguely. I'm making a concerted effort to manage what comes in and out these days. Should you be drinking with that growth in your esophagus?"

"I only have two years left if I'm lucky, and I'm not spending them whiskeyless," he said, putting his feet up on the desk. He wore white running shoes, an orthopedic order. The fat laces looped and hung down over the sides. "Anyway, after the Climate Summit a few weeks ago—there was that demonstration, you know—hundreds of people, mostly students, moved into Luxembourg park near the Sorbonne and haven't left since."

"A sit-in?" I took the glass from him and drank it standing.

"No one knows what it is. They're all just camped out there. It's reached two-thousand people in Paris. And they've spread to Berlin, Barcelona, and London. They're still small, but they're growing. People are packing up their possessions and moving into parks with each other."

"What's their goal?"

"It was ostensibly a response to the climate summit, but now it seems like it's become something else entirely. The point is it's all very strange and there's journalistic opportunity here."

"This is good scotch."

"Think about it," he said.

"You could get anyone for this, Bill."

"I could get anyone, but I want you. Your work on the storm was inspiring. We can develop this more over the coming weeks. I'm packing up my desk by the end of the month. I'm a lame duck and this is my last executive order, so to speak."

He led me through the office floor to a bank of elevators. We paused at the doors, watching the roman numerals light up across the brass panel.

"Remember when I first hired you?" he said.

"We were at that party Knopf threw downtown."

"You were with your girlfriend at the time, what was her name?"

"Celia. That's right."

"I remember you went on about Zola—about how he risked his life for truth and justice, about his willingness to go into exile to defend a persecuted man."

"I still keep his picture above my desk."

"That's why I want you to do this, Paul."

The doors sprung open. He squeezed my shoulder.

"I'll think about it," I said.

I took the subway downtown to see Lena Halley. Not in any great hurry, I allowed myself to wander a bit. I took the line to the east side and then went all the way down to the base of the island before switching trains and heading back up again. These perambulations charged me—watching the bundled commuters swaying like livestock in the whining rollicking overbright cabin as clots of blue light streaked passed the windows. I took my cues from Baudelaire, who spent his days wandering the streets and lingering at cafés, who understood that the contemplative currents of modern life undulated between the inside and outside worlds, between flânerie and thoughtful solitude. But even he would have a hard time keeping up in New York. The city tyrannized you with its abundance and you were forced to match this with the flow of ideas.

Lena lived a few blocks away from the Trade Center, in a new cluster of glass highrises that seemed to have gone up all at once and almost overnight. I took the elevator up, a swift chute. Across the Hudson, the sun slipped behind a factory landscape, becoming something chemical over Jersey. Uptown, I saw the steel-ribbed spire of the Chrysler, the sunburst pattern on its vault, the machine geometry and the jagged faces of opalescent glass, which held the light like a mirror. I could have been a man in a Romantic painting, standing above the smog. Before there were skyscrapers, poets and thinkers alike went into exotic landscapes to find these panoramas. But I didn't think of myself in the same vein as the Romantic poets, going out to discern the hieroglyph of Nature. I believed rather, like Socrates, that because trees and rocks couldn't speak, they weren't able to teach you much, and if you wanted to learn anything you had to live in the polis.

I typically saw Lena the first Monday of every month. This was how she liked it—an organizing principle that offered our promiscuity the thrill of calculation and the texture of conspiracy. We conducted our time apart in radio silence and made it a rule not to learn too much about each other's lives. For her part, she only wanted to know about my past. She asked me questions about childhood, about school: who was my first-grade teacher? What was her haircut like? How did she discipline people? She devoured these isolated historical facts because they added a greater depth of detail that enriched our engagement without the illusion of intimacy.

Lena was, first and foremost, my financial advisor. Since I was entirely ignorant (and happy to be ignorant) in matters of money, I thought the wisest decision would be to pay somebody money to tell me how I should be using my money. I also felt it was good to keep contact with all circles of life in New York, financial types included. If the writer's rightful place was in the ivory tower, and not the tide of shit that surrounded it, as Flaubert contended, then at the very least I should be sharing some of the champagne with its current occupants.

Whereas I knew nothing, and cared to know nothing about high finance, Lena was well-rounded and literate in matters of art and culture as well as capital. Even in New York, you couldn't accuse the Wall Street crowd of philistinism. Many of them had touched Joyce or Proust at some point in their youth, or written an essay on Prufrock in college, and some had even retained the vocabulary from their literature courses (I once had a conversation at a party with a hedge fund manager who told me all about the "negative capability" of the market). Like many people, I was incapable of understanding what exactly Lena did for a living. It seemed like kind of the work that appealed to the paranoid imagination—trades and bonds all day long, figures as good as abstract math, whose fluctuations had world-ruining consequences if they went too far into the red, and I couldn't help envisioning these little sums hurtling through space, riding on light, rounding off and fractioning under blue skies before being sent down into data vaults and memory banks across the globe.

She stood at the marble bar, still in her work shirt, hair up, leaning over a tablet with a mason jar of gin in her hand. With these visits I never knew if I was coming for sex or financial advice.

"You're late," she said.

"Some kids lit up the panel in the elevator. I've been on my way up here for the last fifteen minutes, stopping at every floor."

"You should have messaged me. You know how much I value punctuality, Paul."

"Not possible," I said. "I'm having one of those days where I'm refusing to check my phone out of some vague protest."

"I'm going to tell you right now that we're not going to fuck," she said.

"Did I do something? Is it my stocks? Have you lost all respect for me?"

She stood back and tucked her left instep inside her thigh, making a yogic tree.

· 29 ·

"I could only have had this arrangement with someone I respect. You should know that. We've had a good thing, Paul. But we can't keep this up. I can only take so much frivolity. We need to be responsible people."

"It's responsibility I need a break from," I said. "These little evenings are wonderfully distracting."

"Which is exactly why I won't ask you to get serious."

"You're assuming I can't be serious."

"You're plenty serious, believe me, but not about anything here on Earth, it seems. We only see each other a few hours a month, and even then, I get the feeling your head is somewhere in the clouds."

"We are in the clouds," I said. "Look around you, we're practically in the Platonic realm."

"That's what I'm talking about."

"I'm resisting the temptation to ask."

"There isn't anyone else. Not yet, at least. And it has nothing to do with that."

Lena was a lovely woman: olive skinned, chestnut haired, fine, dark and curved, her complexion luminous, her waist firm and lovingly convex, like the gibbous moon. A moneyed girl from the British Isles, she had the charm of a bygone era, like a woman from the cinematic past.

"Stop describing me in your head," she said.

"You can see it?"

"I can almost hear it."

Her voice had the cadence of a 40s movie star, full of throat and swerve.

I poured myself a drink and she went to the bedroom to change. The flat was lined with floor-to-ceiling glass, and we were so high up that you could look outside and see nothing but sky. It was a separate ambience. Not even the noise of the city made it up here.

"I have food coming," she said. "Stay for a bit, will you? I should tell you how your money is doing, after all."

"I can't take any more bad news today, Lena."

We ate Thai food out of clam containers and watched a TED Talk about smartphones and the ethical use of technology. The speaker described how digital devices were manipulating our psyches and turning us all into information junkies, searching constantly for news and updates and messages the same way people who sat at slot machines did, hanging on the silver arm until they shit themselves and turned catatonic. He closed by saying that he knew of "no bigger problem," because this was the problem that encompassed "all other problems"—useful framing, rhetorically, for an audience that had probably spent all day attending talks dedicated to exposing "problems" that desperately needed their attention. Anyone who'd ever worked at an NGO or any other issue-mongering organization (which TED essentially was) knew that little issues didn't sell. You need a big issue. People needed a unifying theme and a clear formulation they could devote their mental and financial energy to.

The throbber spun and another video autoplayed, this one by a sleep scientist, a somnologist, who talked about how most people on average were getting less sleep now than they were thirty years ago, and how there had been an overall decline in the quality of people's sleep throughout the Western world. He cited spikes in heart attacks and car crashes during daylight savings time and described the phenomenon as a "silent killer" and an "epidemic." (Who knew? We were having epidemics everywhere, it seemed, even in our sleep.)

These were the culture's informants, the issue-makers, a gainfully employed sector in the market of ideas. The genius of any individual, after all, was no match for the genius of the market that made geniuses into commodities. From them you could learn just enough to form an opinion about anything in fifteen minutes or less. And I had: I was suddenly stricken with the fear that I could die from a heart attack or a stroke at the age of thirty-three due to my recent stretch of insomnia.

I knew that "issues" constituted the primary intellectual preoccupation in the culture now, and that this had almost totally displaced philosophical learning. Modernity had left metaphysics and questions of the Self behind, embraced treasure and technology, and concerned itself entirely with progress and problem solving (Alexis de Tocqueville was the first one to point out this feature in American society). It was the job of people who had been left behind, like me, to worry about it, while those belonging to the new world, like Lena, simply got along with it. She was far too busy with mobility and materialism to dedicate much time to abstruse thought. Like so many Americans, she no longer needed the arts and the humanities to brace herself against the perils of existence. And what did this say about people like me, who did? Were we simply incapable of cutting along with the rest of society, which had figured out how to live without it? I was unable, even as I looked out over the capital of the Western world, to find an answer to this question.

After dinner we had another drink and Lena briefed me on my financial status. All good, she said. A bit of a dip in some of the investments due to the storm a few weeks back, but things would rebound.

"You told me you'll be coming into some money soon?"

"I have a friend who recently made a hit film," I said. "I loaned him some money to help him finance it. So, I'm waiting on my return."

"That's great. What are we looking at?"

"Not sure. Enough to help me relax, hopefully."

"We'll find a way to put it to work for you."

She gave me a hug at the door.

"I guess I should get some sleep," I said.

On my way back uptown, Karen sent me a picture from the night of the flood. It was me on top of The Whitney. My face was grey, long, my eyes darkened by blood vessels that lived too close to the skin. I didn't like looking at photos of myself, mainly because they conflicted with my own self-image: the face I saw was always different from the face I saw in my head. It never looked like the face that was doing the thinking.

When I got home, I drew a bath and considered the possibility of a great essay, an overview of the sickness of our time, a supreme work. Every century had its ills. And all of them had their great documentarians. The nineteenth century had its characteristic malaise (Baudelaire saw to that). The eighteenth (Rousseau). The twentieth (Matthew Arnold, a century early). And now I was thinking about my own. Was it possible to diagnose only two decades in? Had it taken shape yet? Since the storm, I'd been waiting to have a Dover Beach moment, standing on the cliffs overlooking the sea while the tides rolled in, a premonition welling up inside, seeing the whole century stretch out before me.

If the masses were truly camping out in the parks of Europe, and spreading to every city, then something was seriously wrong indeed, something beyond what any of them probably knew. What was it? Well, that's what I was going to find out. Something was needed, some insight that could reconstitute the will and galvanize people toward some decisive shift in consciousness. I dallied a bit with other thoughts, and then called up some footage of the sit-ins in Paris. There were people with signs and flags, but none of the rumble and clamor you'd expect. There were some speeches being made, some chants and song circles, but no real incitement of discontent. I saw a college girl wearing a t-shirt that said, "Fuck Capitalism," her cheeks streaked like a linebacker. The protests had taken the form of encampments. Overall, there wasn't much going on, just shots of people sitting, eating, reading, browsing on their phones, kicking around soccer balls with no sense of urgency. I'd expected to see scenes of hysteria and outrage, tantrums, people lobbing bottles at riot shields and screaming beneath their bandana'd faces. I switched over to the newsfeed and read articles for the next few hours, then got on social media to see if anyone was tweeting about the events in Paris, but there wasn't much, not yet. I kept at it for what felt like hours, scrolling down, into endless dead information, going back previous weeks, far beyond any relevance, but it didn't seem to matter. The internet had transformed life into an all-consuming-Now, where everything was buried and nothing would ever die. I felt like I was in Borges' Library of Babel, wandering *ad infinitum* amid all potential realities. I happily lost myself in it.

Jim and I usually saw a film on Sunday afternoon. He needed to spend at least an hour a week in the dark. This was how he spoke of theatres, in enraptured religious terms. They were temples, places of fevered congregation and iconic images. Lincoln Center was doing a month-long retrospective on Fellini, and they were screening *8 ½*, a singular work of genius that we both agreed could not be replicated, a film that documented a moment of crisis for Fellini, mid-life or otherwise, when the director was totally bankrupt—romantically, spiritually, creatively. We sat in the second row (Jim felt the screen should fill your field of vision) as the reflected black-and-white images filled his dark glasses, which he wore everywhere, even in theatres. He was slumped low in his chair, his feet on the seatback, his fingers at his mouth in the shape of a steeple. Fellini originally intended for the film to be about a writer facing a creative impasse, presumably unable to develop his next novel. But Fellini had an uneasy relationship with writers—those whom he knew in Rome's bohemian scene considered film to be an inferior artform. This is actually dramatized in the film, as a critic follows Guido around, waxing intellectual and editorializing his inability to bring his vision to life, telling him that the film "lacks a central conflict or philosophical premise." The decision to change Guido's character from a writer to a filmmaker apparently came after Antonioni released *La Notte* (when *8 ½* was in development), in which Marcello Mastroianni plays a writer in a state of debilitating ennui, uninspired, and stuck in a lifeless marriage. The ending of *8 ½* always stayed with me: Guido, fleeing a swarm of journalists, crawls under a table and shoots himself. In his closing monologue, he confesses his desire to make a film with total honesty, one that would address some essential truth and "bury all those dead things we carry within ourselves." The hope that his muse, the ghostly Claudia, will descend and "create order" is ultimately denied. In the film's closing moments, the critic reemerges to tell him: "In the end what we need is some hygiene, some cleanliness, disinfection. We are smothered by words, images and sounds that have no right to exist, coming from and bound for nothingness." The film ends with a comic inversion, with empty pageantry, when the characters join hands and dance around a sawdust ring, mocking the ideas of resolution, communion, and happiness.

I explained all this to Jim as we left the theater. We walked downtown, the city unrolling like a blueprint. It was late in the afternoon and the breeze was nice. These were the last days of long luminescence, when saving the daylight seemed like literal instruction. Our walks began as a peripatetic exercise, a chance to bounce ideas off of each other and test their durability.

Jim was enjoying a period of recognition after the success of *The Blue Calendar*, his first feature film. Like me, he'd been a critic for years, and was now finally moving into the creative field, because he didn't want to be "a useless critic who never does anything" (his words). Closely based on his failing relationship with his girlfriend Eleanor Blue, it was a biographical drama, and, in its way, also a crisis film. Documenting your own life was an endeavor the culture was promoting at the moment. Everybody wanted to hear about you and your story. Memoir, autofiction, and biographical essays dominated the literary world, and no one seemed interested in other people's imaginations. So Jim took the autofiction concept and applied it to his life, just as Fellini had. He made the film with real dialogue, based on real conversations and real fights. He scavenged his life and put everything into a work of art with a thin narrative persona that everyone seemed to see through, and although the film had been a success, he was being blasted by feminist critics for using his girlfriend's life for material and turning her into an *objet d'art*.

"You know, they're calling you a misogynist," I said. "One critic called the film 'a classic male fetishization of womankind. The work of a domineering intellectual who is incapable of seeing a woman as anything other than his muse.'"

"I know what they've been saying. That's not what bothers me."

We stopped at a crossing, stalled amid tall towers and a road crew churning atmospheric haze.

"I think I fucked up," he said. "I kind of don't want anyone to see it. None of it worked."

"But it's critically acclaimed."

"Critics don't know anything. They all follow each other, you know that, Paul."

"We're not having this conversation again."

"You know, I actually called the studio a few weeks before the premiere and told them I'd do another two films for free if they would just throw this one in a locker somewhere?"

"You spent years on the thing."

"I spent my relationship. At a certain point it became like therapy. The screenplay was a series of updates on how things were with El and I—every fight, every evening at the dinner table, I poured all of it in. Then when the new fights came, I'd go back and rewrite the script. It kept things going. El always knew I was building a film out of our lives, but I don't think she expected any of it to make it onto the screen. Neither did I."

"And what does she think about the whole thing?"

"You should know, you talk to her more than I do these days. She's always on campus, hiding from me in the library."

"We haven't touched it, actually."

"We're not exactly at our most communicative right now," he said. "You reach a point in relationships and conversation just fucking stops. You come to know each other so well that you no longer have to rely on language. Eleanor and I can sit in a room and tell each other everything by the way one of us pulls out a chair or sorts through a spoon drawer."

We didn't talk for a few blocks, Jim's gaze was somewhere ahead, fixed on something miles away. We walked the length of the West Side, the same route I'd taken with Karen in the aftermath of the storm. I took to my surroundings and assessed how everything had returned to normal, or whatever normal was now, in this late autumn light.

"I have my suspicions about success," he said. "I prefer to be out of favor with people. It forces me to work harder, to care more. What I would like to do is make a film that people hate, so that I'll want to win them back."

"Well, now you can finance the biggest failure you like," I told him. "How much has it brought in, by the way?"

He smiled, slightly annoyed.

"I don't know. They send me checks and I don't open them. I'm supposed to be fabulously wealthy, though." He lit a cigarette and let a globe of smoke hang before his face before pulling it into his nostrils. "Don't worry, you'll get your return, Paul."

I was a co-financier of *The Blue Calendar*. A few years back, I received a generous fellowship from a well-endowed and lesser-known council for the arts—money that I planned to take a year off with in order to write a book, a project that never materialized. Jim, who was struggling to fund his film at the time, asked if I could lend him some capital to finish the project, with the promise that I'd get my money back and then some, if it did well.

We walked through a bustling market, peeling off onto a street lined with elms and crowded storefronts where shopkeepers came from doorways, heaping garbage into pickup piles. Occasionally Jim would be approached by someone and we'd have to stop. I kept a little ahead and let my thoughts mingle with the scenery: the hanging elms and the marble arch at the entrance to Washington Square Park. The inscription on its attic read: "The event is in the hand of God."

"Don't pretend like you're not just a little bit happy," I said, "I know that after all these years of being a critic it must be nice to get some good reviews yourself. And to have your face out there."

Every magazine and newspaper in New York wanted to do a profile on Jim, but he was turning them all down, on the basis of them having rejected him back when he was a critic looking to publish his work. Jim had an elephantine memory for almost every slight he'd ever received, and seemed to have an infinite capacity for grudges, so now that the gatekeepers suddenly wanted a piece of him, he was telling them to go fuck themselves.

"I know you'd like to have your face in the news, Paul, but not me."

"Is that so wrong? That's where we should be. Writers have lost their position in public life. I long for the days when you could find authors and critics on primetime TV. Remember when Gore Vidal debated William F. Buckley? Go further back. Hemingway was on the cover of TIME. And Byron was mobbed in the streets because he was such a star. What excuse do we have for losing this status? It's our fault. We've given up, surrendered and gone into retreat. We need to be a part of society again!"

I'd gotten myself so worked up that I'd moved into a speed walk and left Jim standing on the other side of the street. I'd been making long bounding strides, shouting at the air in front of me, crossing the road in the middle of a green light.

We pressed forward, on the raw nerve of the avenue. At Houston we came into the sun and I saw the Frank Gehry building above a rank of roofs, its steel folds waved with light.

Jim didn't want to talk about his film. Like the rest of us, the culture had conscripted him into talking about the news and he wanted to vent about a speech the president made earlier in the day from the rose garden of the White House.

"I don't even want to be paying attention to this," he said. "Because it's so stupid. It should be irrelevant. But we have to because we can't give this fascist an inch."

Fascist was a term he used for almost everybody he disliked. Jim was a talented hater, and his hatred sharpened and energized him, as Goethe advised. It came from the headlines, the newsfeed, the daily updates; he gathered it all and put it in the service of his furious intelligence. Eleanor once described him as a man mad at everything, brimming with world rage. But it was necessary to fight the almost hysterical energy of bigots and big money, he said, government corruption, and the iniquities of capitalism. How else could one survive, especially in a place like New York, without such exalted and exacting contempt?

His moral intuition was that of a child's and he formed his opinions reflexively, out of disgust or revulsion, out of knowing what he hated. He barely read, and when he did, he got most of what he needed by glossing forewords or introductions. When we went to bookstores, he would scan the shelves and read the last page of the titles that intrigued him. He learned so that he could steal. And he was a brawler, physically and intellectually. He once chased down someone who'd stolen Eleanor's purse on the street in Miami. And later, when his turn came, and some mugger pulled the old hand-in-the-pocket trick on him, he challenged the man to show him the gun if he truly wanted his money, before stepping around him. One evening, he even corralled me into defending a prostitute who was being roughed up across the street from his building. I left the scene with a torn shirt and a bruised jaw and a sense of having performed the duties of a chivalric citizen.

An hour later we were drinking on a patio downtown, a long stone slab catching sun. Charcoal pigeons with oilslick necks bobbed about our feet. Jim reclined in his chair with his dark glasses and rolled-up sleeves and elegantly receding hairline. His phone lay between us, the voice recorder running. We'd been documenting our conversations for years in case we ever wanted to revisit them for material. We were also unintentionally capturing other people's conversations, which kept interrupting my thoughts. Their swarming commentary kept popping up, stopping me mid-sentence, so that I had to contend with what everyone else was saying, what everyone else was thinking.

Jim shook his head. "Something has to be done," he said, leaving me to figure out what this meant.

The city was tense, abuzz with nerve and urgency. People looked beleaguered. Whenever you made eye contact with someone you got the kind, muted, and empathetic nod you usually receive at funerals. Everyone wanted to ask, "how are you holding up?" and "are you doing okay?" The flood had caused billions of dollars in damage and the consensus was that the mayor's office had failed catastrophically; his approval rating had reached its nadir and people were calling for him to resign. The federal government had also failed to provide adequate aid to the city in the succeeding weeks, yet another shambolic display in the corrupt, grotesque carnival of error that was the current administration, which everyone (at least in this city) seemed to agree was a dictatorship and that the president himself was a pathological liar, narcissist, and of course, fascist—a fact that, terrible as it was, could only occupy a fraction of your consciousness these days.

"The culture is exploding," I said. "Look around you, people are exhausted."

"You look exhausted. Like you just got out of a POW camp."

"I haven't slept in nights. How can I?"

"How long since you've been laid?"

"I think my gums are starting to recede. And not that long."

Jim lit another cigarette. When he wasn't smoking, he dragged on the air as if he were stealing it.

"People in cities are having far less sex," I said. "I read an article about it a few days ago."

"And why is that?"

"Part of it is option paralysis. People have too many choices and they're oppressed by abundance. The other half of it is demographics. Most major cities have an imbalanced ratio of men to women in the same age group. New York is especially low. There is something like 92 men to every 100 women in this city. We're all swirling around and can't seem to line up our genitals."

"Maybe you should get out of the city for a bit," he said.

"I need the city, Jim. I need the faces, the crowds, the traffic, the sense of relevance."

"You're like that poet, what's his name? You can't enjoy a patch of grass if there isn't a subway under it."

"Karen's invited me to stay for a weekend at her uncle's cottage out on Long Island. But I'm afraid if I leave, I might die."

I considered telling him about Bill's illness, the growth of malignant tissue on his esophagus, his resignation, and the assignment he'd given me, which had been marinating in my subconscious, but Jim was already on to other topics, his outrage in full bloom, because just last week a black man had just been asphyxiated to death on the sidewalk in front a grocery store in Queens, after the cop held a knee on his back for almost ten minutes. The police had received a call for a disturbance (it still wasn't clear what the disturbance was) and the man, who was intoxicated at the time, apparently resisted arrest. Someone had recorded the whole thing and the video was being replayed on the news *ad nauseum*. And now, in addition to the matter of police brutality and excessive force, people's reaction to the video and the position they'd taken on it itself became part of the issue—was indeed an issue itself— because how could people not be in unanimous agreement about what they'd seen? Comment sections were filling up with endlessly unfurling fights, there were split screen arguments every evening on the news, classes were being cancelled out of solidarity, and protests were spilling out into the streets. Jim told me he was actually headed to Brooklyn to meet up with a local chapter of some social justice group that was going to petition the mayor's office to defund the police. On my way back uptown, I saw a sit-in at Grand Central. There were about fifty people huddled in a close circle with their heads down. One person stood above them and spoke while the others kneeled and intoned the same phrases over and over again, as if in prayer.

When I got home, I decided to start thinking seriously about the question—the possibility—of an essay on these strange demonstrations. I dallied a bit, pulling books from my shelves, searching the tags and underlined passages and marginalia, looking for an inspiring line, something with aphoristic resonance. Then I went about sorting my desktop—a scatter graph of miscellany. I dragged and dropped, sliding the sky-blue folders across the cool tableau, becoming a little addicted to the crisp scrapping sound of the virtual trash emptying. I did each piece one by one. I checked my recently viewed: a tutorial on how to fix a stopped sink, a speech the French president had made in Paris commemorating the end of the First World War, a page from the OED on the etymology of the word "escutcheon," a list of the all-time home run record holders, a drum solo, the Wikipedia page on the Spanish flu pandemic, stills of slim smoking girls in French New Waves films, an essay comparing the state of America to the Weimar Republic—for some reason I'd searched the town of Białystok in Poland. I cleared the history and watched it all disappear. I went deeper into my caches and found a graveyard of old news stories I'd bookmarked for reasons I could no longer remember, things that seemed urgent at the time and were now totally irrelevant: an article about the ongoing senate hearings to approve a new supreme court justice, which was being blocked; a scandal involving the sexual harassment of a Hollywood actress (something I'd likely intended to write about and hadn't); a piece on whether or not the president would withdraw the U.S. from an international climate accord (something we all knew the answer to now). It gave me a sense of dislocation, of being out of time, and it was odd reading these articles after the fact, seeing what everybody thought would happen, and how wrong they all turned out to be. The half-life of these stories had been a week, maximum. All that mental labor, all those words spent, and now here they were, bound for my trash bin.

I played footage of the Paris encampments in the background as I did this—cleaning, downloading and organizing all of the material Bill had given me. Garbage in, garbage out.

Gradually, this material began to form its own constellation. I felt like Seneca's Bee, drifting from flower to flower, letting my cells swell with nectar—gathering, digesting, fermenting all of it, then spitting it back out into the world as a new substance. Or, in another, more theatric sense, it felt like detective work, the kind you sometimes see in crime thrillers: a man alone in a room full of crisscrossing threads tacked to suspect photos and newspaper clippings, looking for the linchpin.

Exhausted, I poured myself a drink and stood on the small, gated ledge outside my window. In the road was a large tanker truck with a reclined white cylinder on its back, out of which ran a series of hoses, feeding down into a hole in the blacktop that was surrounded by a small wooden bungalow. Above, ConEd men in orange vests hung from the face of a building on window washer belts like tiny Day-Glo insects. A few gathered around the hole and watched, while another stood at the back of the truck. The hole beneath them seeped a pearly gas, breaking around their boots and slipping through slats in the shed. I noticed that these black tubes were pumping liquid nitrogen. Their ends ran up with knobs of ice that formed links along the hose lines all the way back to the truck, the motor's valves and flanges all encased in hoarfrost. It was possible they were working to repair some damage done by the storm, or it was some routine maintenance, or maybe something to do with fiber optics. It was a mystery to me (how many times in

Advance Reader Copy

my life had I passed construction crews and thought nothing of them?) and I consoled myself with Hegel's reminder that what is familiar to us *(bekannt)* is not necessarily what is known *(erkannt)*. And if I chose to investigate it, it would likely reveal a deep field of knowledge previously unimagined. There was so much to know about everything. What could I do? I was surrounded by more knowledge than I could use in a hundred lifetimes. Montaigne once remarked with dismay how Diomedes had produced over six thousand volumes on the subject of grammar alone. That was in the ancient world. What would he think now? We had more words in our pockets than the Library of Alexandria at the height of its collection. And we lived in an age of non-stop commentary and analysis—with books built out of other books, articles written in response to other articles, which themselves were responses to other responses. The Fourth Estate was now the only estate, as Oscar Wilde said. It had eaten up everything else and become the whole of reality.

I thought maybe my next essay could address all this, in one form or another, and that perhaps our current mania, while ostensibly about other issues, was in fact a symptom of a wider derangement brought about by technology. I decided not to think about it further, in order to keep it a perfect, mental ambition, untainted by real effort. In any case, the thought of turning it into a coherent argument seemed very far away. It would have to be written down eventually, though. Because it wasn't enough to live with this knowledge myself. Everyone else had to know.

I met Eleanor at the edge of campus, in a long, renovated warehouse space that was part-bar, part-bookstore, part-club, part-art gallery, and part a few other things as well, all integrated into a single concept. It seemed like the kind of spot that was made for appearances, that is, the kind of place where people came to be seen—to be seen *seeing*. These types of events were a spectator sport and I was engaging in a bit of it myself. I watched people socialize and then slip away to check their phones, or go to the bathroom to answer a text, or step away to take a picture of the whole room. I browsed the tables and flipped through a book of Helmut Newton's photographs, the glossy nudes and glamourous black and whites—a girl in a rabbit mask, posing on a rooftop in a Manhattan past. Then I took up a book on Romantic painting, which was open to a page displaying Jacques-Louis David's *The Death of Marat*, depicting the murder of the Reign of Terror's great pamphleteer, that vulgar populist who held the public consciousness in his hand during a time of social upheaval and mass derangement. People would open the papers every day, waiting for his instructions; he would call for the execution of traitors and then watch as they went to the guillotine. Thomas Carlyle had included Marat in his book on the cult of hero-worship, along with Johnson and Rousseau as the hero-as-the-man-of-letters. And here he was, in his immortal deathglory, head back, wrapped in towel, naked body pouring over the rim of the tub in a messianic attitude, a limp Christ-like corpse.

I watched Eleanor cross the room, weaving through shoulders and ferrying a plastic cup above her head. She was nearly six feet tall in her flats and the belts of her long khaki coat hung like ribbons, trailing behind her. I made a smoking motion and waited at the bar, where I was quickly conscripted into a conversation with somebody who was going on about the president's immigration policy and a recent scandal involving groups of children being separated from their families and detained in cages at the U.S.-Mexican border. The kid was a few years younger than me (likely a grad student), round-spectacled, mustachioed, Trotsky-esque. He clutched his drink, leaning over the bar, his head down, hands gathered about his chest. I pointed out that this likely wasn't the first time that families crossing the border had been detained—that previous administrations had almost certainly done it too, and that the last president had a fairly unsympathetic immigration policy as well, and had actually deported more illegal, or undocumented immigrants than any administration previous. I wasn't disagreeing with him, or even suggesting moral equivalence (he seemed to take this as whataboutism); I was simply trying to provide some context that could help us understand the situation, but my failure to acquiesce totally to his indignation was taken as disagreement, and the very introduction of this information seemed to offend him, and he told me that this was actually a lie, and he rifled off some statistic I'd never heard of and whose accuracy I was inclined to question because I'd never heard of it. In any case, we both seemed in possession of two separate sets of facts, making this remarkably fast disagreement already unsavable. He said that if I wanted to know the truth, all I had to do was read such and such an article, written by somebody, somewhere. This was the standard response now. Everyone was constantly telling you to read this, look up that, and "do the work."

I was mercifully relieved when Eleanor came and found me. We slipped away and had a cigarette on the fire escape, overlooking the campus with its broad lawns and seagreen roofs of oxidized copper. It was evening, and in the distance the Hudson trembled and threw back the glare.

Eleanor pressed her body against the iron bars, her fingers working the black cage. In this light her face was perfectly radiant, lunar, framed by a lush tumble of mahogany hair. I watched her extract a cigarette from the package with her mouth, pinching her lips around the white tube. Her top lip was a thin pink blade that hovered above her teeth, which were always on display (the term for this, I learned, was "labial incompetence").

"What was that all about?" she said.

"Nothing. We were just talking about the news."

"What else is there to talk about?"

"Thanks for rescuing me, El."

"You looked like a shipwrecked sailor."

This made me think of the storm as I looked out over the river. The tides had receded, and I found that I now remembered very little about the night of the storm, only the words and images surrounding it, only my thoughts, and even these

· 51 ·

were fleeting. They too had faded into a milky collective memory, and everyone seemed to have forgotten about it.

"So nice of your friend Karen to invite us to the cottage for the weekend," she said, lifting her hair with the back of her hand and sweeping it to the other side, exposing her neck.

"You sure it's a good idea, all of us being under one roof?"

"Are you worried?"

"All I do is worry, El. It's how I make my living."

She smiled, looking out over the rooftops. Eleanor's gaze was heavy, dreamy-sentimental, and at the moment she seemed lost in some weighty deliberation.

"Does he ever ask about me?" I said.

"In what sense?"

"Like does he know I'm here right now?"

"He knows I'm with you, yes."

"Well, should I expect wrath?"

"One time he almost ran over this guy from one of my classes because I danced with him at some party. He got the car up onto the sidewalk."

"This makes me feel good."

"Don't worry, he's not going to kill you," she said. "If anybody's going to be in trouble it'll be me."

She asked me if I wanted to stay for a silent disco, the type of event where people listen to music with headphones instead of acoustically, locked inside the closet of their own experience, together but alone, which seemed like a Dadaist experiment, or something the Situationists would come up with, a performance-based commentary on our mediated experience, but Eleanor told me it wasn't performance art, or a comment on

Advance Reader Copy

anything, but just something people did now, and she didn't understand how I didn't know this. In any case, it sounded like something I didn't wish to stay for, even just to observe.

We walked across campus, the evening rose and gold, an owl-light dying fast over the buildings and sharpening them into silhouettes. We passed the library (where Eleanor practically lived these days) and we looked up at the Greek names carved in hard capitals over the colonnade. Eleanor was getting her PhD, writing about love in the Western world. She asked me to help advise her on her dissertation and we'd been meeting regularly for weeks to bounce ideas off each other. I'd been doing my best to stay away from her and was failing spectacularly. Eleanor was lightspeed beautiful and in her physical and intellectual prime. Twenty-six, the age she just came into, seemed to be the age at which both reached their apotheosis. Newton had discovered the laws of motion, optics and gravity by that time, Einstein, the relativity of these laws, Hume had already produced a draft of his *Treatise of Human Nature*, Keats had already produced enough poetry for a lifetime, and then died.

My affection for Eleanor was Greek, which is to say, as attracted as I was to her sexually, what attracted me most was her pursuit of truth. Eleanor, who was well versed in the Greeks herself and in the history of love poetry, told me I worshipped too devotedly at the altar of sex and thought. I didn't dissent from this. After all, *The Symposium* showed that *Eros* and the pursuit of truth were intimately connected—that longing was an essential part of the *daemon* that drives us to know the world, and I wasn't about to shrug at this, or cynically dismiss it, as some critics did. Eleanor too understood that it was no coincidence that sexual and intellectual maturity (which she was determined to get her share of) coincided in the academy, for to be truly educated required the exploration of both frontiers, and it was this literal *lust* for knowledge that Socrates tried to instill in his students, or so I explained as we crossed the zebra on Broadway and headed east, feeling a slight elevation and clarity of mind, as I always did when I was with Eleanor.

In Aristotelian terms, these were the twin peaks of being, and the human spirit chased truth across its latitudes. I'd tried to find a synthesis between the two, which at times could be beautifully confused. I remembered my first year in the city, taking the bus back through the Lincoln Tunnel one evening with a girl from an entry-level Psych. course, and the thrill I felt when she pointed out that the tunnel we were about to enter was a vaginal symbol. I didn't know if it was some ascension of being, or the forecast of losing my virginity that had manifested itself so lovingly in this image. Higher education and higher pleasure came together in this *coitus intellectus*, as the bus's long steel frame smashed through the sodium lit maw.

We walked through the treelined streets, along rows of terraced brownstones, the lamps all coming alive in a unanimous protest against the night. I encouraged Eleanor to riff a bit and I listened to her elegant improvisations on Western love poetry. She told me something about the Greeks that I didn't know, which is that much of the love poetry from the Alexandrian and Roman period was pederastic.

"There is some nymph chasing" she said. "But most of it is old men pining for nubile young boys. Lots of descriptions of ripening penises. Of course, this was a culture where actors used to wear long leather phalluses that would flop around between their legs when they performed comedies. By the time you get to Christian Rome, though, all that disappears. Shakespeare was the first one to write about boy-love again."

We talked about Aristophanes' story from *The Symposium*, about the cartwheeling androgynes who were split by Zeus and doomed to wander the earth in search of their other halves. Eleanor quoted what some critic (she couldn't remember whom) had written (in some book, the title of which she couldn't recall) about how the men who believed in this myth looked for truth everywhere and could find their other half in every tree and every cloud—every encounter becomes an engagement.

"That's you, Paul."

From the bed I watched her move between the bathroom and the window. The orange cherry of her cigarette glided through the dark. She opened her purse and stared into it as if it were bottomless.

"I usually have condoms in here," she said. "Jim hates using them."

"Do me a favor, don't say his name."

"Bad form?"

"It'll hurt performance. You carry condoms around all the time?"

· 55 ·

"They're something you just have, like a flashlight or a screwdriver. Besides, I don't know who you've been fucking, Paul."

"No one."

"Not Karen?"

"We have a friendly, quasi-professional relationship. We're like the Roosevelts."

"In any case, you're wearing one."

She found the wrapper and held it up triumphantly. She came to the edge of the bed. I placed my hands on her waist.

"So, like you were saying."

"Right, well, love poetry is associated almost exclusively with men," she said, stepping away, "but people forget that the genre was invented by a woman. Sappho's poems are among the oldest documents about the psychology of love and the condition of the mind under its spell. It all goes back to her. She was the first one to let people inside her mind, and she laid out the genre's motifs—the pining, suffering, self-flagellating nature of unrequited desire. She showed love as a cycle of tortured pursuit, gratification and then deflation. These are tropes that poets would adopt and develop for centuries."

She was standing before me now, a pale boney girl in her flats. She parted the trench coat, revealing herself to be totally nude underneath. Had this been the case the whole way home? She went to the bathroom before we left and she hadn't been out of my sight since. The lapels hung like curtains beside her breasts and framed the dark inverted triangle of her pubis.

"The point is, the type of masculine consciousness we associate with love poetry—the kind some female critics disdain—actually has feminine origins."

"And what type is that?"

"You should know Paul. You're one of them."

"I once wrote a love poem to a girl who sat next to me in the fifth grade. It was a single quatrain, as I recall. Think that was my last crack at it."

She was on her haunches now, straddling me at the midsection.

"The types tend vary by country," she said. "English poets tend to be devoted, monogamous—Spenser, Donne, Tennyson, Arnold—they all celebrated the virtues of married life. The French on the other hand have a curious lust for whores, syphilitic mistresses, and randy teenagers—think Baudelaire, Verlaine, Rimbaud. There's a lot of scatology in French poetry too, descriptions of filth and odors."

"Very French, yes."

She worked at the zipper on my pants.

"But then there's the Petrarchan type, where the pursuit of the woman is allied with the pursuit of truth. Sidney's sonnets are examples of this, as well as Shelley's *Epipsychidion*—it's a type of enlightened beauty that gratifies the intellect.

"Well, didn't Shelley write "Ode to Intellectual Beauty?""

"*Hymn* to Intellectual Beauty. And yes, he did."

"So which one am I?"

"You're the last."

She tore at the condom wrapper with her teeth.

"But most of these women never knew they were the subject of so much scribbling."

"No, they didn't," she spit a strip of foil on the bed. "That's a key—the mutual ignorance. The author never fully understands the one they're pursuing. And the pursued almost never knows they're being pursued."

I said, "It's about conquest and understanding."

"Don't try to conquer love with your understanding, Paul. The moment you conquer it you'll kill it."

She raised herself up. The condom hung on her thumb like an umbrella.

"I guess we should fuck now," she said.

After she lay next to me, coat open, her small breasts flattening at the edges. She moved her hand over her torso, making little depressions with her fingers and tapping out spots on her abdomen like a drywaller trying to find a stud. I pressed my cheek against her stomach, listening to the troche of her heartbeat and the little grumblings of her inner tracks. She rose and walked to the bathroom, picking up the bedside lamp by its neck and bringing it along with her though the dark. Infidelity, stomach pains, the way she got up to piss in the middle of the night. If someone were to write a comprehensive biography of her life, these would be the details that would go up for editorial debate: how much of this do we need to see? Is this essential information? Does this really need to be said? Years of being the subject of her boyfriend's work left her feeling that nothing in life was spared. Everything was documented, captured, and made for public viewing.

"That's what happens," she said. "A woman's stomach sounds in the night and the next day it's in a movie. Consider what we're doing right now."

"I'm considering it."

"We're having a moment."

"A clandestine moment, an intimate moment."

"It's just another thing waiting to be news. That's how it goes. Two people meet at midnight in a dark room and have a moment and the next day it's the world's business."

"Come here," I said.

"People love having moments. And they love creating them and talking about them before they're even over. They say, 'look at this moment we're having.'" She came from the bathroom, brushing her teeth. "On our first date, Jim took me to a bookstore and bought me a copy of Mallarmé's poetry."

"Some nymph-chasing there."

"He said that everything existed to end up in a book. Now, everything exists to end up everywhere else." I heard her stop to gargle and spit. "Is it weird that I'm twenty-six and I already feel like I've experienced everything? Like everything is a cliché? I'm so bored with the state of the world—bored with myself."

"It's natural for people to think that the world is getting more boring," I said. "The world is collecting material, every day, and there's nothing new we can say about it. It's no secret, the more we live, the more we feel like we've been through all this before. If modern life is so boring, it's because the world has been through all this so many times already. Even the world is bored."

"I avoid taking the subway these days," she said, mouthful of bright blue paste, "because every time I go down there, I see film posters with my doppelganger on it. The whole world knows my business, Paul."

"We all know each other's business all the time," I said. "Nothing hides. There are no secret spaces. Except here, El."

"Let's hope we can keep this secret."

She lay down again, looking at the ceiling with muted animal eyes.

"Don't worry," she said, already on her way to sleep. "He won't kill you."

These nights were like a module that we could both climb into, deep and familiar and lonely, like two all-night technicians at a panel in a basement a mile below the earth who needed each other's keys to launch a nuclear strike. I got up and had a cigarette on the windowsill (does anyone really need to see this? I thought, does this need to be shown?). Outside, a garbage truck worked its way up the street, its spinning amber lamp swept across the buildings. I saw a billboard hovering in the distance on a rooftop a few blocks away, lit like a beacon, an ad for cloud storage, likely, though I couldn't tell—black letters spelled out against a white backdrop, reading:

Keep Your Memories Safe

I woke up sometime in the middle of the night. The room was total darkness. I picked up my phone, still lumbering into conscious thought, opened my note pad and tapped out a few ideas that had come to me from the dream state. Then I opened the news and scrolled through stories. There was a piece about a corporate merger, two massive communications companies coming together. Another story about a pro athlete's infidelity, which substituted a picture of them crying (presumably on the court after losing a match) for the emotion they were likely feeling now, or the emotion the journalist who wrote the story believed they ought to be feeling. There was a story about how warming waters, acidification, overfishing, and tourism were killing coral habitats. It wasn't an article, but a video, roaming shots of the ocean floor, the camera swooping over bleached reefs, a whole aquatic metropolis of dead sponge-like matter. This was intercut with close-up hi-def footage of furry corals flexing their feelers, their little tendrils and tentacles reaching, as the captions (explaining what corals were) ran silently underneath. Then I watched footage of a failed ballistic missile test carried out earlier that day in North Korea: the rocket lifting uneasily from its tower before shooting off and exploding into forking paths of smoke. After the video ended, I left the page waiting with the little circular refresh arrow in the middle of the black screen. I waited until my phone automatically went to sleep, tossed it, and then went to sleep myself, a montage of these images repeating in my head. When I woke again, the light was just rising. I watched Eleanor's sidelong frame for a bit, then I checked my phone and found that the notes I'd taken were nearly incoherent, not even intelligible enough to try to parse.

We left shortly after sunrise, rolling out on twin slabs of blacktop that launched into the morning. We drove out of the city, under tall motorway lights, past slip roads to shopping malls and the backs of suburbs. The skyline receded, crowded in reverse in the rearview mirror. The highway ahead waved like an oven lid. About an hour out we slipped off a frontage road and into webbed developments, with Georgian homes set back into cul-de-sacs, playsets and tricycles scrambled across the lawn, porch lights, newspapers in blue bags leaning against iron gates. Small towns always depressed me. Nothing got me down more than the sight of tackle shops, dealerships, signs that said things like "Slow, Children Playing." Since moving to New York I'd never ventured out to Long Island. It seemed to me to be the kind of place where people went only to die, or die slowly.

It was the worst time to be leaving. The demonstrations, or "the Events" (as they were being called) were going viral and now there were gatherings in nearly a dozen U.S. cities, people camping out in parks and squares, setting up little occupations and refusing to leave. They had popped up with astonishing speed, almost overnight, and city officials had no time to establish perimeters. I wanted to stay in the city, in the middle of the action, but I was overruled. In any case, it seemed that a sojourn to the coast could be productive. I was going to take the opportunity to do some serious thinking about the essay, the protests and everything else.

We followed a coastal highway and came to a field of windmills planted in the ocean; long, rotating rows of propellers arranged like white memorial crosses in a war time cemetery, their ruby and green pilot lights flashing soundlessly. When we arrived, Karen was on the porch, waiting between the newels, drinking and arranging some decorative gourds. She came down the long unpaved lane to meet us, dragging her feet on the stones and calling out, her voice sounding crisp in the expanse.

I spent the afternoon reclining on the porch with a lowball glass and a high state of mind. I brought along my copy of *Crowds & Power*, hoping to review it for some insight, and was unable to make it past the first chapter. It was riddled with notes and marginalia I'd made when I first read it as a student, and I was so embarrassed by where my head seemed to be at the time that I gave up and sent the book cartwheeling onto the lawn. Karen corralled us into playing bocce ball and horseshoes ("When was the last time you got out and tossed a ball, gentlemen?" she said, "instead of tossing books?"). Jim and I faced off against Karen and Eleanor, who were becoming fast friends. I watched their bodies flex and extend as they flung the iron shoes toward the stakes, torsos and limbs outstretched like sketches in some Renaissance book of anatomy. The toenail-shaped steel struck the posts and clapped away into the distance; the light was in the trees, my palms reeked of metal and the air was cool and tinged with sea salt.

Jim and I kept up our discussions by taking perambulatory exercises along the beach. He was reeling about something the president had said earlier that morning, lurching and stammering as he spoke. When he got going, his anger made it into his body and hobbled him. I tried to calm him, but he was already onto other subjects. He'd been in contact with some activist groups in the city who were getting involved with the camps. He suggested we try to rally support for the demonstrations by publishing an open letter in a magazine and getting celebrities, journalists, public intellectuals, and other people of "influence" to sign on—and he wanted me to write it.

"Support for what?" I said. "We don't even know what this thing is yet."

"Exactly. That's why someone needs to explain it. You can do that."

"I don't even know what my own thoughts are."

"Well, sort them out and let's do it." He watched a stack of gulls wheel above the water, his dark glasses hiding his eyes. "Bill wants you to write about it anyway. Ask him if we can do an open letter."

"Bill's leaving," I said.

"He's retiring?"

"He's dying."

Like many people I knew, Jim was being swept up into a life of sleepless indignation. He didn't want to talk about books or movies, only injustices and systemic failures. He felt it was socially irresponsible to be occupying yourself with art in a time of distress, when the stakes were so high, when you so obviously needed to get involved, and he wanted artists and intellectuals to show their worth again. He believed, like Plato and like Lenin, that it was the duty of an educated vanguard to explain the world and organize life for those who couldn't help themselves.

Our conversation spilled over into dinner. Jim sat at the head of the table, leaning over his plate, hands at each side of his face, describing something in the air around his head.

"What's it all about?" Karen said. "I'm not up on what's going on. I've been trying to withdraw from the media out here and it's killing me. I'm carving the days into the wall."

"I can't imagine," Jim said. "It's an integral part of my morning, turning on the news and grinding my teeth."

"We had to see a doctor about it eventually," Eleanor said. "His teeth hurt so much."

Karen poured out the wine. "I spent years of my life living at the same pace as the news. It never stops," she said. "The news is like a train running through the night. And we get up every morning and chase it. Of course, I'm just a photographer. The demands are different. We don't all have time to sit and meditate like Paul."

"I don't meditate, I brood."

Jim was working through his potato. "That's Paul."

"I've always said it's necessary to brood at least one hour a day," I explained. "It's like going to the gym. Daily fitness."

"It shows," Karen said. "You've got that all-night look. The toiling insomniac."

A breeze whistled through the screens and in the living room a few smoldering logs sizzled in the fireplace.

"About these gatherings," Karen addressed Jim. "These 'Events.'"

"Yes, about them."

"What exactly is it you want to do?"

"First we need to think about why they're happening," I said.

Jim took a slug of his drink. "Here we go."

"It's very strange, isn't it?" Eleanor said. "People just abandoning their responsibilities and shacking up in parks together? I feel for them. I don't know why."

"I don't think it's about any one thing in particular," I said. "I think it's a kind of protest against the state of things in general. We're totally overwhelmed by how many issues we have to deal with now and we're just tapping out, like a child lying on the floor."

"You see the London camp was just broken up?" Eleanor reached for the peas.

"When was this?" I said at a volume too great for the room. I was embarrassed that I hadn't heard about it yet. I was already behind, already robbed of some opportunity. I felt the urge to open my phone and post something.

"Just a few hours ago," Eleanor held up her phone. "Looked pretty nasty. The police were merciless."

"I once online-dated a guy from London," Karen said.

"What was that like?"

"He sent me a vial of his semen in the mail. That was that."

Jim raised his hands—"Can we continue?"

Eleanor made a tray of her hand, as if to say, *proceed.*

"I think we should write an open letter, a kind of call to arms, and get people to put their names to it. We need a clearer articulation of what these demonstrations mean. They can only last so long before they have to mobilize and form into a movement. That's why Occupy Wall Street failed. They had no leadership, and they never thought about the next step."

"We need to consider the wider cultural phenomenon," I said. "People are desperate for perspective. They look to journalists to explain the world to them. We're the new priest class and we have a responsibility."

"Blessed are the newsmakers," Eleanor held up her glass.

"Critics can't shape the culture," Jim said. "They can only react."

"And what are you working on?" Karen looked across the table and brushed my leg.

"I've got my own thing," I said. "That Bill asked me to write. It was his last order."

"How is Bill anyway?"

"He's dying."

Eleanor was into her steak now. "This is excellent, Karen."

Jim leaned back in his chair. He stretched and addressed the ceiling.

"The point is you never *do* anything as a critic."

Eleanor spoke into her plate: "Oh my god, will you two stop?"

"You used to be one," I said.

"Is that why you quit being a critic?" Karen handed Jim the spinach.

"One of the reasons. I used to think that writing was a form of action. I used to believe in the power of the critic," he said. "That what is said about something is more important than the thing itself. But I no longer believe in triumphant analysis, the superiority of commentary to reality."

"You want to have another one of those impossible arguments?" I said.

"We've had some epic ones. Remember that time at the oyster bar in D.C.?"

"They asked us to leave."

"I guess we didn't understand the decorum."

"We didn't speak for a week, as I remember. We went back to our rooms and took different trains home."

"Those are hours I will never get back."

Eleanor and Karen smiled through the silence. Jim ashed his cigarette in the remainder of his potato. Then he lit another and refilled his glass and settled himself into the back of his chair.

Eleanor looked up. "I was thinking. What was I thinking?"

"You were thinking how Paul should help me with this letter."

"I can't remember. Christ, ever since I started my dissertation everything else seems to have evacuated my brain."

"You're really not going to help me out with this?" Jim said.

"I'm working on the big one," I said. "The one people remember you for."

"I'm not asking for much here. The least you can do is use that intellect of yours in the service of real-world matters. You have a chance to be useful. Just don't drone on about this Hegelian 'crisis of world-consciousness' stuff that you've been unloading on me every time we talk. People won't understand that—let alone rally around it."

"You underestimate the role of the moral imagination in determining real-world change."

"Fuck you and your imagination."

"Alright." Karen leaned over and began collecting the wine bottles. Eleanor was in the middle of a coughing fit and she was waving her hand, trying to pacify Jim.

"You know it is possible to disagree respectfully," I said.

"Oh fuck off."

"If you'll let me explain—I'll need at least three minutes."

"Nope."

"History is accelerating and so are we. More things happened in the twentieth century than any century previous—everything from the atom bomb to cellophane. Christ, it feels like we've lived through a lifetime's worth of events in just the last year. Did you know there was a coup in Myanmar last week? And the week before that there was a mass shooting in Finland? We should still be talking about these things, having serious discussions, but we're not—because new things keep coming at us. We don't have the bandwidth!"

Advance Reader Copy

Jim slid back his chair, colliding with Karen and causing her to drop a clutch of plates on the floor. Eleanor threw a roll that bounced off Jim's shoulder and tumbled into the living room.

"You're an ass, you know that!"

"It's fine," Karen said.

"I'm sorry, Karen."

"Don't worry about it."

Jim swept his leg under the table, gathering shards of ceramic with his foot.

Eleanor followed Karen to the kitchen. "I'm going to come and live with you from now on, if you don't mind."

I pushed in my chair.

"Don't think I'm letting this go," he said.

Karen came back with a broom and started sweeping up the shattered dishes. Eleanor stood behind Jim.

"Get up," she said. "Go do something."

"He knows I'm right. That's the problem."

"Right."

"He can't stand agreeing with me."

"Yeah, yeah."

He took the dustbin from Karen and folded the plates into a newspaper.

"I'll take this out," he said. "I'll get more solidarity from the racoons."

Then he was gone. The spring door swung and banged against the darkness. I put some more wood in the fire and lay on the couch. Karen stood at the sink and Eleanor at the threshold of the living room.

"Well, I think that's as good a time as any to call it a night," El said.

Karen went around the veranda, collapsing the shutters, a briny maritime air moaned through the doors and the slats and the skylights and I heard the soft fall of Eleanor's feet in the bedroom above, she and Jim talking in low tones. Around the living room were odd articles in pocketed shelves—carved wooden things, souvenirs from vacations, beer steins filled with beach glass, sun-blighted photographs of twelve-year-old Karen on fishing trips with her uncle, the old morality of home life, family and memory.

Karen came from these locales, the melancholy nautical towns where the foot of America gave way to Atlantic twilight. At eighteen she left for good, looking to "collect experiences," as she put it. She got a job working for a photo blog where she did insane assignments, like hopping a freight train and taking it across Siberia, recording her whole journey. She photographed coal miners in Romania, gypsy ghettos in Rome, the Arab spring in Egypt; she saw a building collapse on a twelve-year old girl in Lebanon and stood over the rubble to get a shot of her father pulling her out ("I've always felt shitty about that," she said); she shadowed prostitutes in Mexico City, spent a weekend drinking vodka with Albanian gangsters and documented the pederastic nightlife of the Tokyo underground. A month ago, she was in the Philippines, where she saw a man get stoned to death during a riot, standing a hundred feet away, a girl with her camera, watching as the blunt objects laid themselves into his skull and left him on the

Advance Reader Copy

road waving his hand at everything around him. They kept on kicking him even after he agreed not to move anymore and she was pretty sure she saw the moment he died. A week later she was in Japan, where she took a photo of a blind man on the street holding a sign that said: "I can't see you, but I love you," and twenty-four hours later she was with me in the streets of SoHo, ankle-deep in the high tide.

She said, "This is probably the most time I've spent in one place in—I can't remember how long."

She climbed on the couch with me, slow and groaning. Her hair was up in a bright elastic and her face was the same color as the clouds at thirty-five thousand feet.

"I started drinking at noon today," she said. "That's acceptable on Saturday, right?"

"That's why people come out here. In the city it's still socially unacceptable to have a glass of wine with lunch, even among the liberal-minded classes."

"You sound like Jim."

"Speaking of whom."

"Don't apologize," she said. "Nobody got hurt, so let's just fucking forget it."

"We've had some pretty good rows in our time. That was minor."

"You're like a family, the whole damn bunch of you. And I feel like I'm being pulled into your orbit. I'm trying to avoid situations, Paul."

"That's the second time I've heard that this week."

She crossed her legs and the pale skin of her knees came through the rips in her jeans.

"What does he want from you anyway?"

"He has this idea that I'm a lifetime collaborator. I only helped him out with his first film because he couldn't afford to make it on his own. And I offered to read the script for it because he didn't trust anyone else. Naturally, I learned all about Eleanor."

"She's something."

"She is. Few women have the effortless charisma she possesses. What did the Italians call it, *sprezzetura*?"

"Only you would know something like that."

Karen was tender and candid. She had no guile, no artifice. She didn't care what people thought about her and it was this earnest, meaning nature that drove so hard to the heart.

"I'm amazed the two of you are even friends," she said. "Aside from sharing that woman you don't seem to have anything in common."

"Excuse me?"

"I know, Paul. I can practically smell her." She sank her fingers into my neck and put them to her nose. "Yep. You'll need to shower again."

"Look, Karen."

"I won't ask you to explain yourself to me."

"Maybe you should, maybe that's what I need. To describe the contours of my psyche."

"I haven't asked you to make any commitments, Paul. And I know you're not capable of it. That's why I like this. We have our little thing."

"You should be in that chair," I said. "And I should be lying here, looking up at the ceiling."

"Just be careful. The shit is already at shoe-level."

She mumbled stories while falling in and out of sleep, fragments and half-sentences from a dream state. She carried time zones in her mind, the sound of jet engines slept in her skin. She told me that her greatest fear was "not living enough"—whatever that meant (maybe it meant a series of memorable events that collectively constituted some sense of passage, or what we liked to call "experience"). But she'd done the math and realized that she'd spent the bulk of her existence in hotel rooms and terminals—long periods of profound non-experience—and she was always in a hurry, reading while walking, trying to finish a paragraph before reaching the bottom of an escalator, or seated next to old women on night flights, trying to think of a conversation that could connect her to a person she'd never meet again. "You're the first person I've had a real conversation with in a long time," she said. "It's nice. I miss it." Her relationships were with her subjects: the village kids in the Congo who scrambled about her legs, looking to get in front of the camera, tugging at her pockets for a bit of American candy, the kinds of people she could only say "hello" and "thank you" to, the people whose lives she'd come to capture but would never know, like the Buddhist monk in Cambodia who hadn't spoken or left his chamber in the ashram for eleven years. She didn't know how to function in one place for any more than a few days in the absence of work, and she didn't know how to not take pictures of things (she even captured our horseshoe game earlier in the day). I suggested she take the advice of Pascal, who said that all of humanity's problems stemmed from our inability to sit alone in a quiet room (advice I should have taken more often myself), to silence the nagging voice of the other Self that always wants to be somewhere else, just out in front, in the future, anywhere other than here.

Karen drifted off to bed and I poured myself another drink, happy for a lone moment. Then I took one of Jim's cigarettes and stood at the back door, smoking through the screen. You could feel the pressure dropping. Another nor'easter was climbing the coast, but this one was en route to head back out into the ocean. I felt a touch of sand on my feet as the wind moaned throughout the house. I took it as a metaphor: the world leaks in.

I pulled out my phone and checked social media, which was trending with videos and images from the ransacked London camp. I saw crowds, bodies making a human barricade, trying to hold the ground, and there was someone on top of a squad car, a boney kid kissing a bullhorn, middle finger to the air; then there was scramble of limbs, close-ups of faces fighting for the frame, people throwing rocks at riot shields, tossing back smoke cans, and I saw wild flailing forms, a shattered storefront and a boy being dragged away with a bloody skull. It was a large-scale tantrum, glorious and demented, a scattershot of human misery. Here finally was an expression of what I felt had been lurking underneath these demonstrations. Clamor. Mourning. Angst. A violent outcry of accumulated anguish, rife with transformative potential.

And then it came to me, the idea for the whole thing, in one timeless flash: the piece that could address the culture and diagnose everything that was happening and why, a commentary that would capture public attention, the kind of thing people would be reading on the subway and walking around the city with, holding it above their heads, proclaiming: "Yes, this is it! This explains how we feel!" All the undescribed anxiety, the collective anomie, the political disenchantment—all of it could be unpacked. "Yes!" I shouted, marching a few paces and throwing a haymaker at the air. Again, the sensation washed over me—the acuity, the coherence, the understanding, the almost coital lucidity. I paced the room back and forth several times, not knowing what to do or where to go with all this insight. This was it. Yes, I thought. Yes.

I looked over my glass into the mirror behind the airport bar. Bill Morning was passing through LaGuardia, on his way to somewhere, and he wanted to catch up. From my seat I had two television screens available to me (the only time I ever seemed to watch TV was in the airport): one fixed to a skirt that came from the ceiling and ran the length of the bar, and the other, a large composite display in a lounge area outside that was caught in the reflection of the mirror, along with the bodies of luggage-bearing travelers being conveyed across the concourse's huge interior. Many of them stood on the motorized walks, dumb and unmoving, their heads following the screen, which showed footage of a wildfire that had broken out somewhere in northern Alberta, engulfing huge swathes of boreal forest. The scene was apocalyptic: a wall of ambient orange light above a landscape of dark spruces. The city nearby was being evacuated. I watched all of this in reverse. The TV directly above me ran a cable news program, a split screen tête-á-tête between two pundits, or "analysts." The volume was low and the close caption bars popped up above a crawl that contained other headlines and a counter showing fluctuations in the DOW. I took it all in. Amongst the interplay of visuals, machines and shifting masses there was in addition my own reflection, an object among other objects, no more or less significant, afloat in a field of noise.

"I love airports," Bill said. "All these people, coming and going. The feeling of *intersection.*"

We faced forward, looking into the mirror like horses in our stables. I was interested to see him again partly because I'd expected him to have undergone some kind of atrophy in the intervening weeks, the loam of the grave already on his shoulders. Instead, he had the healthy windburn flush of a sailor, a pouchiness and girth that gave him an added confidence and dignity, as if he had grown into his illness and absorbed it. He had also let his hair grow out somewhat, wearing it messily with a carefree attitude.

"We just came from the outback," he said. "We went on one of those walkabouts, you know, where they make you hunt and kill your food. You're supposed to wander in the desert and have some kind of hallucination."

"Did it work?"

"Didn't see a damn thing. I don't think I followed the instructions properly."

"I think it requires drugs," I said.

"Elsa and I bought some peyote from a Vietnamese kid in our group. But we didn't take enough. I haven't been high in almost thirty years."

"I've heard some Wall Street brokers do it at the end of every year to reorient themselves. Like an annual cleanse."

His feet rested on the brass rail beneath the bar. He was in shorts and deck shoes, with no socks. A relaxed traveler. At ease in transit.

"You look good, Bill. I can't believe it."

"Neither can I. We've been to five countries in the last three weeks," he said. "We're trying to hit all the places we've wanted to see for years. Elsa also has an agenda of finding me a cure. She did a bunch of research online about alternative medicine and holistic healing. Last week I was sleeping with a rhino horn. Before that I was taking some cocktail of honey and ginger. I'm drinking zeolites now."

"What are those?"

"They're a type of crystal forged in volcanic explosions—I think. Apparently, they have a symmetrical molecular structure that's rare in nature, and this is supposed to be good for all kinds of ailments."

"Sounds like a load of shit to me," I said. "Where'd you find that?"

"You can find it online. They send you a whole kit. You're supposed to grind the rocks into a powder. If it's not of the correct fineness though, the crystals will shred your insides, like a spoonful of glass."

"Like during the Black Death. Eating emeralds was thought to be a cure."

"Anyway, you can mix it with stuff. I've been putting them in shakes," he said, rattling the canteen next to him. Inside a collapsible spring ball stirred the pearly contents.

"Is it working?"

"I don't know. I'm trying everything, accumulating treatments, mostly to appease Elsa. I don't really expect anything to come of it. The tumor is inoperable and she didn't take well to my decision to refuse chemo, so she wants me to try to wipe it out all together with a miracle cure."

In the mirror I watched Bill's irongrey eyes open above the canteen as he raised its nozzle to his mouth and sucked at the stem. He winced slightly as his throat pumped the sick pink substance down.

"Where are you at right now?" I said.

"Well, I'm making preparations to live and to die. Which is a strange place to be in."

"Have you thought about where you want to be buried?"

"Lie in the ground? No way. And forget about donating my body to science. I don't want to end up on some metal slab while a bunch of trembling med students slice me up. I want something memorable. I've been thinking I'd like an airplane to scatter my ashes in the atmosphere." He nodded at the tarmac. "Or I could catch a ride on a space shuttle. They can dump my ashes in orbit and I'll circle the earth every ninety minutes. Or they can fire me into deep space. Maybe I'll get picked up by intelligent life."

Bill ordered a beer and cheese sticks. I was leaning into my own overpriced tuna wrap.

"Have you ever heard of the NASA Voyager mission?" I said.

"Which one is that?"

"They sent a spacecraft out beyond the solar system—this was back in the 70s—and equipped it with a disc, like a gold record that contains a cache of information that would give any alien life a picture of human civilization."

"Right. What's on it again?"

"Coordinates to our solar system, bird calls, people saying hello in a hundred different languages, photographs, images of people in an everyday kind of way, some Mozart, some rock music. Humanity in a nutshell."

"See, I would love something like that. They can put my whole genome on a record and play me out to the universe."

"The inevitable death of the universe doesn't bother me so much," I said. "I've always thought that the greatest tragedy will be the day when there's no longer any record of our existence, when everything we've ever created will never be seen or heard from again."

I tipped my head back and finished my beer. Over the balcony I saw people being ferried through skywalks and escalator banks, standing under huge displays, waiting in serpentine lines.

"How's the essay coming along?" he said.

"Oh, you know, it's coming."

"As your editor I'd say I have the right to read it."

"If you were still my editor."

"Carol will do a wonderful job in my place. Be nice to her."

"I've always liked Carol."

"So, how close are you?"

"I have my idea and it's developing in a big way."

This wasn't exactly true.

"Give me some pages. Just the opening paragraph. The abstract. I want the thrust of it."

"You'll read it when everyone else does," I said.

Through the window I watched aircrafts drop in over runway pylons, each rolling through a lonely spot in the cloudlet, trailing cumulus in their wake—a double-deck 747 with bowed wings, a small shuttle craft and other commercial airliners, all dragging delayed roars in their approach.

He said, "I assume you've been to Central Park then?"

"I was down there the day the bodies piled in. They came in columns, bearing sleeping bags on their shoulders. It was remarkable."

"Elsa and I stopped by the camp in Sydney. They seemed lost."

"The New York camp is now the largest," I said. "Paris and Barcelona shrunk in the past month—people had to get back to their lives, I guess. But this one is growing every day. It's going to approach critical mass soon."

"Which is why I wanted to meet with you," he turned to face me. "I was contacted last week by one of the organizers of the Paris camp. He was under the impression that I'm still an editor. He's relocating to New York and he wants some publicity for the camps here."

"Is he a leader?"

"I'm not sure what he is. But I gave him your name. Thought you two would have plenty to talk about."

"Can I call him?"

"I think he prefers to meet in person."

"Listen, Bill, I have my own thing going here and I'm really not interested in whatever some French neo-Marxist culture jammer has to say about it."

"I have it here," he said, taking his phone out. "He told me he wants to get in contact with the leadership here in the city so that they can organize, coordinate. That's one of their biggest problems, apparently."

"They have bigger problems than that, believe me. Existential ones."

"You can ask him about it."

"He should talk to Jim. He's in 'the leadership.' Did he say anything else?"

"Not really. He wasn't a very loquacious fellow. How's your French?"

An overhead announcement sounded somewhere distant, volleying unintelligibly through the space. I added the number into my phone.

"What's my obligation?" I said. "I'm sure he didn't select me because he likes the way I round off a sentence."

"No obligation. I'm just trying to help you out. Might give you something to think about."

"I have plenty to think about, Bill."

We walked through the concourse. Sunlight collected in the vault above, a ribcage of glass and sloped steel, pouring down onto the floor of the terminal. Families washed out from all-night travel were collapsed in the seating areas, sleeping on their luggage. A group of stewardesses passed by in their blue uniforms, nylons and neckties.

"What will you do when you're done with this article?" he said.

"Start the next one, I guess. There's always the next one."

"Never stops," he said. "You might want to focus on your future. Have you thought about the next ten years?"

"What the hell else am I supposed to do?"

"Children. Some responsibility, maybe. My father used to say that you're not a man until you have kids."

"I hear people say things like that."

"Take an associate teaching position somewhere in a warm climate," he said. "Grow vegetables, BBQ on Sundays and watch the kiddies run around the lawn."

"Slow death," I said.

He laughed.

"Oh. I'm sorry, Bill."

He checked his phone. "I have to go. It's good to see you, Paul." We shook hands. He could sense I was pensive. "What is it?"

"It's nothing. It's just—how does it feel?"

"To be dying?"

"Yes."

"You should know. We belong to an industry that has one foot in the ground. Isn't that what we hear every day—the death of the author, the death of print, the death of journalism? You want to know what it feels like to know you're dying? You and I have been living the lives of dead men for years."

The essay, the commentary, the great explanation, whatever, had been gathering mass in my mind over the past few weeks, dragging itself along behind me everywhere I went like a fish net, and now I needed to cut it open and let it spill forth onto the upper decks of my consciousness. It needed to be completed, and soon—people wouldn't sit in Central Park forever. I also now had some devotion to Bill. I felt it needed to be finished for his sake as much as mine. It was he, after all, who insisted I take on the project, he who bequeathed this task to me upon notification of his death, and I guess in some way, I owed him (this must have been what someone—I couldn't remember who—meant when they said that man's ability to realize himself was strengthened by the passing of others). But Bill was still in the spring of his senescence, still walking around with the deceptive ruddy glow the living unknowingly wear.

It began taking shape. Since starting, I'd produced tens of thousands of words of burn material and several dozen drafts in an attempt to locate my organizing theme. It was now my main *idée fixe*, the lattice through which I viewed everything. When I went out, I saw thematic potential everywhere—tissues formed with every encounter. I would go downstairs to get a coffee, hear a conversation standing in line, and feel that in some way it spoke to what I was working on. I came upon possible epigraphs at every turn, every word uttered on the subway became quotable, significant.

I was fairly indifferent to the political dimension of these "Events," and viewed it merely as a rhetorical overlay that concealed a far deeper, less diagrammed concern. I'd considered several approaches to the topic—political, ideological, economical, anthropological, etc.—but all of them terminated at something far more spiritual, you could say. After all, these social and political paroxysms were, in Hegel's view, fundamentally a problem of individual self-consciousness on its way toward some actualization, attempting to reconcile itself with a kind of world-consciousness. It seemed to me that these occupations were the perfect metaphor—no, a real-life demonstration—of the ails of modern consciousness. Here was an embodied angst, the groping clamoring populace expressing their unwillingness to continue with things as they were. You could plug in any issue you wanted—government corruption, environmental degradation, income inequality, racial inequality, patriarchy, the deranging effects of new technology—any of them would fit. It was all of those things and it was none of them. Thus, I set about to write an exploration of the alienation, anomie, *weltschmerz*—whatever you wanted to call it—that defined our time. These gatherings illustrated just how inundated we'd become. We were all living through

Advance Reader Copy

what felt like major historical events every single day, too numerous to absorb, and it seemed as if we were accelerating toward a great self-actualizing moment, or at least the ghost of one. This consciousness was bound to boil up, spill over, so that a massive democratic cry into the void was the only outlet left for our grief.

In a way, I had been rehearsing the essay for years, in my head, every day, in the shower, standing in lines, on subway platforms, waiting for trains, in the backs of cabs, in the mental interstices of our daily routines. The problem was that the subject had always overwhelmed me—it was simply too large a concept to contain. Before, I could never conceive of a fitting or coherent framework on which to hang all the ideas that I had been developing. Now, the prospect of a global sit-in, a worldwide time out, provided me with a packaged opportunity to confront the subject head-on.

These thoughts, among others, came to me while soaking in the tub. I decided to take the Archimedes approach, drawing contemplative baths, losing myself in the hopes of reaching a "eureka!" moment. It was an old-fashion model, with porcelain paws and a rolled rim, and positioned with a view of the Midtown skyline, now towards sundown, the layout of its buildings resembling newspaper columns. Vapor trails from jet engines grew and settled into bright blades across the sky, which had turned the color of cotton candy. I knew that Bill was on one of them, lifting and falling through the soundless hemisphere. I tried to visualize all that air traffic, the overlapping navigations, the ribboned flight paths, stratospheric routes all measured out to the minute, which, when seen from space, would streak the seas and block out whole continents.

I reclined and opened the tap with my toes. Water poured through the metal mouth, filling the room with the smell of wet copper. I thought of Marat, shoehorned in his medicine bath, lined with chemical foam, his skin peeled red and raw, his elbows daubed with oatmeal, a tray across his lap. I draped my arm over the acrylic lip, letting my head fall from my shoulders and adjusting to a lazy posture.

I lay there, teasing at epiphany. I wanted to capture the clouds, hug the horizon, anthologize the moment and hold the whole thing in my head. I thought that at the very least maybe Leibniz was on to something in believing that the clock of the mind, though separate from the world, sometimes chimed along perfectly with it. But this only came about in moments of real understanding, which most of us, in our lives, only flirted with. If you had any duty in this life as a conscious thinking thing, it was to capture and transmit this understanding out into the world so that others could take it up for themselves. I thought my essay could do this. I wanted to produce one real thing, put something out into the universe that would not degrade, but shine through and state, without apology, without irony or guilt, something around which people could gather and say, "yes, this helps us."

I'd been going down to the park almost daily. The camp, sprawled across the length of the Great Lawn, was visible enough from my perch on the fifth floor, and I would look out and observe it throughout the day as if it was some disaster, a public-health calamity that people had become accustomed to and were ready to ignore, like homelessness or bombed out buildings. The camps had become part of New York life, and the life of so many other cities. They'd been growing steadily over the past few weeks, but the sense was that they were peaking now, that pretty soon they'd flatten out, lose their appeal, and from there it would only be a matter of time before these defectors ultimately returned the manageable fraudulence and thinly spread malaise of late capitalist life.

The Great Lawn had been turned into a shanty town, a bivouac. It reminded me of a similar settlement the people of New York had erected on this very spot in the months following the stock market crash of 1929. They built bungalows of scrap wood and corrugated steel and began living in the park, cooking food over fire barrels and getting water from public mains. These settlements sprang up all over the country and became known as "Hoovervilles." I'd seen pictures of the New York camp in a book Karen had at the cottage (*The*

Great Depression in Photographs) along with the soup queues, the sandwich lines and the dust bowl children.

But this encampment was entirely different. Most people seemed in good spirits, and more interested in documenting their participation in it than actually being a part of it—whatever *being a part of it* meant. They were posting, streaming, updating, podcasting, and everything else (I heard the word "viral" a lot while walking around), and everybody seemed intent on being noticed, looking for photo ops and chances to get their picture in the news. The previous week, *The New York Times* ran a cover story featuring a photo of a kid carrying a sign that said, "The Revolution Will be Streamed." Once identified, he quickly became a face of the movement. He'd already collected over 50,000 followers online and was being interviewed in a number of magazines. The media was looking for answers, understandably. So was I. I spoke to people every chance I got, asking them where they were from and why they were there. I usually received a different answer from each person. One of them, a kid studying philosophy at Columbia, told me that he was there because of systemic racism; a group of young women, also students, told me it was about "the patriarchy." There were also plenty of environmentalists. Some of them were career activists, people who lived with the smell of gas in their nostrils and advanced on every G8 and climate summit. Someone told me it was about "sticking it to Wall Street" and that this was the sequel to the Occupy movement. The word I heard most was "inequality"— everything was about some form of inequality. Another unifying theme was that everyone seemed to agree the president was a fascist and that the United States was descending into dictatorship.

Sometimes Karen accompanied me to take photos. She had an affinity for runaways, the dropouts, the drifters and the drug-addicted kids. These were her subjects, after all. She documented the lives of strays, exiles, the meek and the extreme. She'd been to enough refugee camps in her day that she knew the business of talking to people and asking about their stories. And this was a refugee camp, in its way, a temporary settlement for people who were opting out of the demands of civilized life. But it wasn't full of dread, a little misery pool where people sat around sulking. It was rather, surprisingly festive, an atmosphere similar to the night of the flood, a bit carnivalesque. Everyone acted as if they knew everyone else, suddenly friendly, the automatic connections formed by shared place and common purpose. I confess I didn't understand it, and I tried not to involve myself too much. I felt I needed to be slightly removed from the phenomenon, an observer, maintaining the clarity of a critical eye.

The next day I got stuck on the subway. I'd been shuttling around all afternoon, on various insignificant business. At some point we stalled between Brooklyn and Canal Street Station.

We were likely somewhere under the river. People seemed for the most part undisturbed and went back to reading or playing games, faces down at the tablets in their laps. Occasionally, I would catch reactions. People would chuckle, sigh, roll their eyes, or mop their faces in dismay. They all looked bored. What were they thinking? I thought, as per my conversation with Eleanor, that reading the news encourages us to think that the world is getting worse, because it's a constant series of updates on things that are going wrong; but the world never gets any better or any worse, I'd said, it simply gets older—the world just knows more. The corollary of this, I thought, is that it should get wiser too. But I felt the world wasn't just getting older. It was getting fatter. It was accumulating more and more junk every day and it was becoming increasingly difficult for us to get around. Every minute, every second, more items were being added to the great mass, the great quantity of things to know, things to think about and things to rob you of your time. Soon the people in the car became impatient, a sense of animal panic setting in. One man yelled "Come on!" I looked over at the screen of the woman sitting next to me. She was reading the BBC. The page was notifying her that she had updates and was prompting her to "pull down to reload." I watched her manicured hand perform the action. Her bright nail touched the screen, the page drew down and bounced. But it failed to refresh. It kept prompting her and she did it a few more times, becoming more and more annoyed with each finger stroke. Finally, it said: "Error loading page. Please try again later." I thought this should be the headline. This is what we really needed to see. I wanted to open *the New York*

Times the day after a major disaster and read: "Thinking About It, We'll Get Back to You." At that moment the train came to life. It lurched and took a curve. The rails screeched and we all leaned into each other slightly. Those standing with their hands on the straps made a wide stance and balanced themselves. At the next stop half the cabin emptied. People spilled out onto the stilted platform and disappeared down the stairs. When I got off a few stations later, the woman next to me was still going at it, pulling down and watching the little pinwheel spin, each time failing to deliver.

I met Lena Halley downtown for lunch. I wanted to preserve some semblance of friendship between us now that we weren't fooling around, instead of contacting her only for cold financial advice. We sat on a leafy patio in the sunlight next to the tall flames of gas-powered torches. It was one of the many restaurants in the square where her office was located, a galaxy of glass polygons near ground zero and the entrance to the Staten Island Ferry. Lena had just come from a meeting with some very high-profile clients, where "a lot of money changed hands." Just imagining what this might have entailed made me anxious. She sat across the wrought-iron table in black stockings and a glaucous-colored skirt, her hair up in a business

Advance Reader Copy

beehive. She asked me what I was up to these days and I gave her a vague, evasive answer. About the essay, I was teasingly oblique. I'd become superstitious and thought that talking about it before it was finished would somehow contaminate the effort. "I've got this thing I'm working on, you'll see," I told her. The pavement of the courtyard burned white in the cold afternoon. Out in the river I saw the orange-long body of the ferry, the floating waiting room, carving its white way through blue waters. Our food came and Lena told me not to start eating until she took pictures of our plates. I asked her how my money was doing and she waved her hand at me while chewing as if to say, "fine, fine." In truth, we didn't have much to talk about. She said she was seeing someone from her firm, a guy who worked a few floors above her. She reached across the table and showed me photos from a trip they'd just taken to Morocco—the two of them on the beach, in the marketplace, standing in squares in front of mosques and minarets. All the photos had a sepia tone to them, which made them look much older, from a more distant past. It was instant nostalgia. Instant distance. She showed me two identical photos, asking me which one I preferred. I said I didn't know. She lost herself in this decision for a few minutes. I did the same, making a few notes, unrelated to the essay—just things I thought were worth putting down. We sat for a while in silence, embracing the pleasant indifference of commuters: a mid-day rush, patios packed with crowds, bits of jargon hanging in the air, trade language and legalese. The people came and went like variables in some mad statistic. Then we said goodbye. Instead of going home right away, I decided to do a bit of Baudelairean exercise, wandering the city and making passing observations, with no real sense of direction, or at least trying to have no sense of direction. It was impossible. You could lose yourself in Paris, but not in Manhattan. The city's Euclidean grid wouldn't allow it. Despite my best efforts, I found myself back at the apartment an hour later. I didn't have the energy to compose, so I drew another one of my contemplative baths and spaced out for a while, I don't know how long, until I heard Karen come home.

One afternoon, while drifting about the city, I decided to visit Jim at his studio. He'd been in Los Angeles the previous week for a film festival, doing some press for *The Blue Calendar* and also getting involved in the camps there. He tried to persuade the actors, directors, and the press to boycott, or else suspend the festival out of solidarity for the demonstrations, and a clip of him arguing with an interviewer on the red carpet was getting a lot of hits online: "I'm talking about solidarity— you're talking about gowns and golden idols! You're an idiot!" Though the boycott was unsuccessful, the video of him castigating the reporter succeeded in its way, prompting people on social media to call for the cancellation of other festivals and award ceremonies that season.

He'd also gotten attention for being at the L.A. camp at the moment it was broken up. The night turned violent when riot police used rubber bullets and tear gas to disperse the crowds. Jim sent me a picture of himself from the lobby of the hospital; he had a look of muted pride, smiling with a split lip, a beehive of bandages around his head, and he was smiling a little bit now, sitting at his computer, leg resting clinically on an overturned trash can, as he showed me videos (most of them from phones) taken in the heart of the confrontation.

"Where the hell were you yesterday?" he said. "I called. A bunch of times."

"I was out and about."

"Doing what, exactly?"

"Riding trains mostly, wandering the streets," I said. "I did that for a few hours. I also spent some time in the bath."

"Still with that. What the hell do you do in there?"

"I withdraw into myself. It's nice."

"Well next time you're riding trains or sitting in your bath, just be conscious of the fact that there's real shit going on out here." He scratched at the bandages above his ear.

"How much more conscious can I be?" I said. "Actually, that's kind of my theme. It's something I'd like to talk about."

"You've never bothered with the real world, Paul. The real world can go fuck itself for all you care."

"You make it seem like I live some monastic life," I said. "Did I not sign that petition with you to boycott the Saudi government when that journalist was killed in Turkey?"

"That was an honor."

"And did you not read the piece I wrote this spring on the active, adversarial role the media has to take against this administration?"

He lifted his finger. He motioned to the monitor, where there was footage from the night of the raid: a bound quarter of shielded officers, a clamor of hands and batons, a scramble of fists and limbs. I saw a bunch of people running around with milk streaming from their eyes (apparently dousing yourself with milk was good if you got blasted by pepper spray), screaming and crying white.

"The camp got raided around nine o'clock," he said. "A line of cops filed inside the barricade with shields and nightsticks and started smashing tents and dragging people out into the street. There was a lot of chaos. People didn't know what they'd done wrong."

"What was the reason? Why now?"

"They said the camp had become a health and safety hazard. People were getting ill and refusing medical attention and instead were being treated by med students in the park. There were also some allegations of sexual harassment that I'm almost certain were cooked up by the mayor's office."

"They've been saying the same things here, yeah."

"I don't really remember much after a certain point. I obviously got knocked out. Next thing I knew we were in the hospital. I guess I got clubbed and stepped on a few times. Grade-three concussion and two cracked ribs, Paul."

He unwrapped the bandages, revealing a train of staples running through his hair.

"Jesus."

"It's not as bad as it looks. You know Eleanor nearly hopped on a plane and flew out when I phoned her from the hospital. She said she was already in a cab. I had to argue with her to stay home, right there in the waiting room."

"She worries about you."

"Her nerves are terrible when she worries. She trembles, her knees knock. It used to be really bad when we first started dating. During exam season she wouldn't be able to fall asleep."

He winced as he got up.

"I'm surprised they let you fly back so soon," I said. "Do they let people who have recent concussions fly?"

"Why wouldn't they?"

"I don't know. I know you can't stand or lift stuff or do anything at all for very long."

"It's not like being pregnant."

"Something about the pressure in your head," I said. "Ears popping and all that. Can't be a good thing."

He hobbled over to the window and pulled back the curtains. Light invaded the room, angling against the structural beams. He winced again and blocked the sun with his hand. In the frame of the window, I saw the dark lattice of the RFK bridge, the red diode lights around its towers' steel archways flashing metronomically.

"You haven't even heard my good news," I said.

"And what is that?"

"If it pleases the court: Bill got me an interview with one of the organizers of the Paris camp."

"How does something like this fall in your lap?"

"He asked for me specifically. Why the hell, I don't know. Anyway, I'm going to meet with him to hear what he has to say. Maybe you two can coordinate."

"So when are we meeting this guy?" he said. "This mystery man."

"Sunday. Five-ish.

"Did he say where?"

"Bill gave him my cell. I'm to be texted an hour or so beforehand with a location."

"Clandestine."

"Yeah."

"Well, he better have some fucking ideas about where we go from here," he said.

We continued in this manner as we plunged down the slope of Lexington Avenue with the light leaping at us from the numbered intersections and the wind beating against the seal in the driver side window where Jim held his cigarette. He reached his mouth toward the gap to exhale, straining as he did so. His head was all encased in cotton again, and he'd cut slits in the cloth above his ears so that he could wear his shades.

"You know, you don't have to go out there and get whacked just to feel like you're earning your keep," I said.

"How else am I going to earn it?"

"How far are you willing to take this? Let's say the demonstrations mobilize and become a legitimate force in this country's politics. What will you do, become a strategist, start meeting with congressmen? You're going to have to start carrying a briefcase. You won't like that."

"I'm disappointed you find it so easy to mock people's attempts to fight for their livelihood."

"Is this me mocking? I happen to be in total agreement with you."

"We can't all spend our days lying in bathtubs, Paul—contemplating god knows what."

We parked in front of his building. I decided to walk home, across the park again. I joined the crowd as we packed ourselves under a stretch of scaffolding that ran the length of the block. Men in bright vests worked in the tiers above us, dumping scraps down a blue chute, chipping and sandblasting away.

Perhaps Jim was right that I needed to spend more time with the culture. He had little respect for the prolonged stupor writers needed in order to work. He was too busy going out and getting beat on by the police, boycotting film festivals and berating interviewers for their shallowness, and in turn scolding me for not doing more of this myself. I understood his imperative. I too felt pressured to participate, to be an agent in the cultural drama. If you wanted to be involved, to be visible (as everybody did), you had to sacrifice the solitary pleasures of the imagination: you had to take the afternoon off and endure several hours of seminars and meetings with the local chapter of some social justice group, or you had to pack up your things and go sit in the park like everybody else, or descend on a G8 meeting or a climate summit, where, if you were lucky, you would get your head smashed in so that you could post about it the next day, or wind up in some viral video, and if you got enough attention for this, you might even end up on the six o'clock news, spending hours in an overbright studio for a five-minute segment where they wouldn't focus on the questions you considered important, and in which you were likely to be less articulate than you'd hoped to be, which meant despising yourself a bit for having done it in the first place, and then you would spend the next day rewatching the segment and criticizing yourself while also fielding the inevitable criticisms from other people, who felt you'd missed something or were being "tone deaf," which meant losing yet another day to this clean-up work, and then, if you had a regular gig, like I did, as a final act, you would be required to pen a few thousand words about it for next week, in order to set the record straight—and where, in all of this, would be the time for thinking? Philip Roth said long ago that the news threatened to put the imagination of the American writer out of business, and he was right. The culture was sucking the life out of me and I was trying to recover some space for what someone—I couldn't remember who—termed "cultivated inaction."

But even now, as I ran this through my head, I was back walking through the park, strolling along the waste and colored fabric of the tented settlement. To my surprise I saw Lena Halley and spoke to her briefly. She looked good. She said she was there visiting some colleagues of hers from the hedge fund. The movement had penetrated Wall Street and now even investors were tossing their ties on the floor of the stock exchange and smearing dirt on their faces.

The camp was a little village, a micro-polis. There were cafeterias, medical tents, even a library (I came down one day with Eleanor and donated a few books). They had their own network and research and teams working through the night, people at collapsible desks on computers powered by generators twenty-four hours a day, updating and streaming live feeds from other encampments in cities over the globe, coordinating litanies and silences, holding vigils and lawn symposiums, inviting celebrities and public intellectuals every day to stand on a riser and express solidarity.

Every day at three o'clock, a general assembly was held, a meeting where people could get up, say their piece, report news, make proposals, raise concerns, deal with in-camp problems, delegate tasks and assign duties. Everyone was allowed to speak, and I was surprised to see that no was ever shouted down or booed. Those who organized and managed the assembly were not authority figures, but moderators, and everything was decided by majority vote. Since it had access to the resources of greater Manhattan, it seemed that given the general level of cooperation and peacefulness and overall functionality of the camp, this occupation could go on indefinitely. There were accusations of drug dealing and sexual assault, but this wasn't enough to justify a raid like in London or L.A. The city didn't push it, because they knew that the winter would eventually put an end to the whole thing. Most people seemed to sense this, and over the weeks talk began about the need for a final push, a large demonstration before they would have to relocate, regroup, reorganize, etc.

I said goodbye to Lena and told her I'd call her sometime. I crossed Central Park West and came under the shadow of the Natural History Museum. There was a sign around the neck of the Teddy Roosevelt statue that said: "END IMPERIALISM."

Jim was right. I took seriously the idea that it was the writer's job in a democratic society to provide people with some understanding of their condition, where they'd been, where they were going. Foremost, this meant more time for contemplation. "Read, read, read," Lenin said to his mistress. *Think, think, think*, I told myself. This republic of opinion, this American experiment, demanded it.

I passed the planetarium in its glass case, now lit up, the model planets suspended within.

I'd been doing my share of thinking, sure, but it was all of this kind—thinking about thinking, trying to think, preparing to think. Something was out of order, inside me, or all around. The world had been sending us signs of disharmony: the superstorms, the demonstrations, Bill's illness, the inertness of that unstoppable object Karen Marlowe. Soon the birds would be dropping from the sky and the animals would be eating each other in their stables. But presently, as I crossed the museum's lawn and headed home with the sun in my eyes, the pigeons were still on their stoops and the light was in the sky and the level ocean waters rolled obediently on.

When I came home, I found Karen at the kitchen counter, chopping carrots.

"I'm going to make some soup," she said.

I went to the toilet. On the door handle, waved like a tilde, hung a black bra, lifting in the wind.

"I took a shower earlier, hope you don't mind," she said.

When I came out, she had a glass of some clear spirit ready for me. I sat at the counter with her, curiously exhausted. She was in jeans and a large oversized white shirt, her black hair frayed and straight like a shop broom. I thought she looked like Patti Smith on the cover of *Horses*. A light meter hung between her open collar, its silver chain descending her boney chest.

"Where were you?" I said.

"Out with Eleanor."

"You've been seeing a lot of her lately."

"Oh, and does that bother you, dear? Are you jealous your Eleanor is spending more time with me than she is with you?"

"I just wonder what you do together."

"Oh, you know, just a couple of gals out on the town. There was an exhibition at the MoMA we wanted to see. She's a sweet girl. She's got a kind of Greta Garbo thing going on."

She leaned over and withdrew a paring knife from its housing block. The woman who killed Marat (I couldn't remember her name and was too lazy to look it up) had stabbed him with the same type of knife, just below the collar bone. I'm not sure what made my mind go to this; maybe because Karen had turned on the TV and there were shots of Paris playing on the evening news, sweeping pans of blue mansard roofs and the Eiffel Tower, like a dagger, sticking up through them.

"What's this?" I said.

"They're rebuilding Notre Dame."

It was a bit of good news, a positive break from the litany of shit one usually saw at six o'clock. The reconstruction was still in its early stages. There were shots of a tensile trellis going up around the back of the cathedral, a metal net that would be overlaid with iron and timbre, true to the original design. Then they showed footage of the fire from a few years ago, the flames devouring the interior, the rose window glowing orange, the Gothic spire capsizing and a smoke column spreading across a bronze sky. I remembered watching it live and being more upset by it than any mass shooting or celebrity death in recent memory, and I'd stayed up all night writing about it, but now I could hardly recall what I'd said, and anyway, it didn't seem to matter anymore. Whatever I'd thought, whatever I'd written, was irrelevant now.

We ate our dinner and then sat on the couch, letting the news run on mute.

"How's your little thing coming?" Karen said. "The Great Whatever."

"Don't get me started."

"By all means. I like it when you get started. I've spent years doing most of my talking while waiting in line for something. It's nice to hear somebody ramble on for a bit."

She yawned, stretching out in torpor. She threw her head back, showing her hard jaw and the soft ribbed column of her throat. Karen was lovingly androgynous, bridging the sexes, almost alien, like the ancient species from Aristophanes' story, the cartwheeling moon creatures that roamed the earth before being split in half by Zeus for daring to scale Olympus.

"You got some mail," she said. "Been paying your bills?"

"I introduced a policy years ago never to open my bills because I knew I wouldn't like what I'd see. I figured if the day ever came when I was in serious financial trouble, I'd know about it. A pair of hired goons in repo jumpsuits would come here and start chucking my furniture out the window. Hasn't happened yet. Besides, I have someone downtown who watches my money. She'd tell me if anything was amiss."

"Jim hasn't paid you back for the movie yet?"

"He's got other things going on right now. I'm not about to break his legs for it."

"You can stay at the cottage, if you want," she pinched my legs with her toes "The country air would do you good. You've got raccoon eyes and the haunted look of a recluse. When I first walked in here I half-expected to find you with a long beard, standing at the end of a line of urine jars."

"The country people will be too hostile to me," I said. "They'll know I'm not one of them. They'll see me as a self-improving city slicker, dabbling in a pastoral lifestyle. They'll throw bricks through the window and run me out of town."

"It'll be nice. You can write on the porch. I can start a garden."

"We both know you won't be domesticated. You'll get bored. You'll be running out the door in a month. Not that I mind. It might work, actually. We could be a team—partners, like Eleanor and Franklin Roosevelt. You can be the cultural ambassador, out doing work in dangerous terrains while I stay at home and brood on world crises."

"And what about *your* Eleanor?"

"She could be my Lucy Rutherfurd."

"I'm sure I don't know who that is."

"She was Roosevelt's 'mistress.' By that I mean she came to the White House every couple of months to read to him and rub his legs."

I held her feet in my hands. How was it that a woman like Karen, who'd risen from the status of colleague/acquaintance to part-time roommate in just a few weeks, seemed to fall into the orbit of my life? I'd relinquished all agency in letting it happen, not wanting to oppose the force of circumstance. If the universe dropped a Karen Marlowe in my lap, who was I to protest? I chalked this up to a latent desire for tension, the self-actualizing force that was forged through the meeting of opposites. If it was true that our original sex had been neutered, that we were all incomplete androgynous beings hopelessly wandering the earth in search of our other halves, then it was likely I was searching for the other half of an idea, a full body psychology. But Karen didn't need another half, because she'd already been born whole. She didn't need companionship for completion; she was happy enough out there on her own, her and her camera, cartwheeling around the world.

We walked along the aisles, El and I, fishing for a book that was stashed somewhere in the rosewood shelves, in the dim, dry, lamplit spaces of the library, some collection of literary essays by some obscure critical theorist from the early twentieth century—Kirshner, Kossner, something like that, a scholar who probably thought he'd live forever, climbing into posterity, but now survived only here, as a potential footnote to some digression in a girl's PhD thesis. For Eleanor was writing her own great explanation as well, her theory of love in the Western world, from Socrates to Yeats, from Athens to America, and like me, it was taking its toll on her. She'd been sick for weeks now and was trying to power through her project. She coughed into her hand, a deep heave with wet cracking phlegm. The sound echoed through the quiet room, bouncing off the coffered ceilings. It was almost hypnotic, her chest expanding and contracting, a place I'd loved and explored, charting its contours in the dark.

We stood together on the checkerboard floor. Rows of Ks were stacked in front of us. Most of the names I'd never heard of before (I thought most books in libraries actually went unread). I pulled one out and checked the card in the back, last stamped April 1996. This depressed me. I put it back.

"I used to judge people based on their bookshelves," Eleanor said. "First thing I'd do whenever I showed up at a party. Go and check their books. I once refused to sleep with a guy— who was actually very cute—because of the books he had. I took one look at them and made some excuse about how I had to leave."

"And what was there?"

"Lotta those 'How to Be Happy,' 'How to Get a Life in 30 Days' books, you know. There was also some Ayn Rand."

If the catalogue of one's lovers were a bookshelf, this encounter could be filed under the self-help section. Everyone's shelves would be different, of course, but this would be one of the common genres. There would also be the awkward first reads, rushed and stumbling, ignorant of mechanics and craft. There would be the poets, the singular beauties, the ones you always wanted to go back to. There would be the one-night stands, the novellas you could clean off in an evening. There would be the aborted efforts, the ones with whom we couldn't get past the first chapter. There would be the cheap thrillers, the melodramas and pulp fiction whose pleasures were accompanied by secret shame. And there would be the obligatory reads for a rounded education—the canon, the classics. And on it would go. And if you were to take an overview of this shelf in its early stages the taste would be eclectic, appearing to have no coherent interest or affinity. It would be a monument of discovery, dabbling, dilettantism, pretension, good and bad ideas, things you embraced and then rejected. But eventually a dominant genre would emerge, a body of knowledge you could embrace.

"Men have been making women into books for centuries," Eleanor said, head down, scanning something she'd pulled from the shelf. Eleanor always read standing up. She'd pace her apartment, walking into tables and chairs, stubbing her toe on everything because she had to think on her feet.

"Is that so wrong?" I said.

"It's certainly given us a lot of great poetry."

"And bridges, and skyscrapers, and airplanes."

"If you're so committed to making your lovers into books, just make sure you read them. Don't just let them sit there, accumulating mystery."

We sat at a quiet corner table in the glow of an emerald-headed lamp. In the lobby, I saw the mural depicting a shielded Athena, defending the masses from the devils of disorder. I checked my phone briefly. I received a news notification, but when I went to open the page it got stuck loading, the little rainbow wheel spinning infinitely. It made me anxious. I pulled down again, waiting.

El smacked me on the shoulder. "Here, take a look at these," she said, indicating the pages in front of me. They were the notes on her thesis, the raw thoughts. I picked them up and began reading:

"…In his dialogues, Plato uses his character Socrates to show how longing elevates itself to the level of intellectual contemplation, the nature of which is philosophy itself—*philo* (love) + *sophia* (wisdom), and the goal of longing, in this case, is the unattainable—total knowing, transcendent Truth. *The Symposium*, the clearest dramatization of Socrates' longing, places love at the center of the discourse on how we can come to know the world. 'Love,' Socrates says, 'empties us of the spirit of estrangement and fills us with the spirit of kinship.' Which is to say, a kinship with reality, to understand things the way only god can, to know every wave in the sea and every leaf on the tree. But there is a tacit acknowledgement that this can never be achieved, for the longing for Truth always exceeds itself; it requires an object, a stand-in, on which the love of wisdom can focus itself. In the tradition of Western poetry, this object is another human being, often a woman or a young boy. Plato apparently wrote love poetry in his youth before abandoning it for philosophy, which in practice, meant exchanging the understanding of others for the understanding of nature. The Platonists, escaping from their caves, are not concerned with foreign psychology. They're not interested in exploring other people's caves (this is *doxa*, opinion, which is a threat to true knowledge). They seek rather to study reality, to stand in the light of the sun in order to understand things as they are. Reality itself thus becomes the object of longing. But the Truth must remain hidden, concealed in the realm of 'the forms.' It has to, otherwise the philosopher would be able to capture it, and the game would be over…"

"…Nietzsche, the great critic of Plato, was the only one courageous enough to point this out, appropriately using the analogy of Truth as a woman, and asking if the philosopher had truly succeeded in attaining her: 'Is there not ground for suspecting that all philosophers, in so far as they have been dogmatists, have failed to understand women—that the terrible seriousness and clumsy importunity with which they have usually paid their addresses to Truth, have been unskilled and unseemly methods for winning a woman?' This truly is the philosophy of the bedroom, in which the object of longing becomes clear, identifiable and attainable. According to Nietzsche, not only have philosophers failed at attaining knowledge in the bedroom, it seems they can't even find the light switch."

"…Socrates' declaration of his own ignorance—'I know that I know nothing'—is his way of trying to disarm himself, of installing awareness of incompleteness as the saving grace in the pursuit of knowledge (one cannot expect to know everything). The longing to be educated, which Socrates infected his students with in his dialogues, is the longing for completeness. The feeling of completeness can only be teased at in moments of elevated erotic experience. But whereas sex can temporarily satisfy feelings of erotic discomfort, the discomfort of not knowing enough can never be wholly satisfied. Wonder, the woozy overwhelmedness, is the source of this feeling—Socrates describes it as a kind of madness that approaches the divine. It rushes in to become the dominant expression for both the Platonists and the poets whom the Platonists disdain…"

Eleanor wiped her nose, her nostrils going hot and pink at their edges. She launched into another coughing fit and I heard somebody shush us a few rows over.

"I'm gonna have abs after this," she said.

"Do you really think—" I began.

"Don't talk. Read."

I continued:

"…By contrast, the poet elects the beloved as the object of longing, the source of all the world's wonder and mystery, and the attainment of them means the attainment of the world. The inherent virtue and purity of the beloved (untouched, uncorrupted) and the virtue of pursuit itself replaces the virtue associated with the longing for Truth in Greek love-of-knowledge. In the pre-modern era, this is illustrated most clearly in the poetry of Dante, Petrarch and Sidney; and in the modern era, in Keats, Shelley and Yeats. Shelley, who was more intellectual and had more Socratic skepticism than his contemporaries, likens his Emilia, the subject of his *Epipsychidion*, to the lamp of knowledge, radiating Truth, and he addresses her with Socratic appeals: 'And we will talk, until thought's melody / Become too sweet for utterance.' He doesn't want to get laid, he just wants to learn…"

"…In the case of Dante, his Beatrice is a specter, the ghost or *geist* of ultimate virtue. Petrarch succeeded this by actually selecting a real person on which to hang his desire, and he fashioned an entirely new genre of poetry out of it, one that would dominate love-writing for the next five centuries. As with the Platonists, it is essential that the poet's desire go unrequited. For that is the only true form of love. The pursued cannot know they're being pursued. If they did, the project of true fulfillment would be contaminated, threatened by foreign psychology, something that confounds the poet's worldview. Yeats, for example, makes no effort to understand Maud Gonne; he keeps her at a contemplative distance for fear of being disturbed by too much reality, and his self-flagellating desire is his compensation, the source of his authenticity…"

When I looked up Eleanor was gone. She was off somewhere, following the alphabetic shelves. I heard her cough, clear and crisp in the wooded space. I took out my phone again and tried to reload the newsfeed. The page was stuck. It looked as it had an hour ago. It was a dead page, a carcass. I pulled down again with my thumb. I checked and saw that I had no bars. I looked around and saw others staring despairingly at their screens, likely suffering the same thing. I went back to reading:

"The poetic archetype, to a certain extent, must shut the world out, exclude reality, with all its actions and happenings, in order for the 'inspired condition' to maintain its state of longing. Keats, who accused Newton of 'unweaving the rainbow' was unhappy with more reality, with someone else telling him the truth about the world. Again, pure empiricism threatens longing. A clear, unambiguous description of something takes us out of the realm of desire and into the realm of understanding, which can never fully satisfy the poet's sensibilities. If a thing is understood, it is robbed of its mystery, the generator of all longing. Keats managed a positive spin on this by articulating the concept of 'negative capability'—that aspect of consciousness that is content with not having to figure everything out. This was Keats's way of saying, 'Let trees be trees. What's important is what you think about them'—a notion impossible to permit for the philosopher, who, as Simone de Beauvoir remarked, must be arrogant by virtue of what they seek: the total attainment of Truth."

The area around the text was crowded with arrows, slashes, stars and marginalia, like "Cf. Goethe" or "re Dryden," all written in blue fountain pen, little encoded notes whose cypher only Eleanor knew, the droppings of her mind on the white page at the moment of thought. I added a few of my own notes, in a different color and different-sized hand, all these little fragments conversing with each other on the edges of the document. I read on:

"Finally, the poet and the philosopher came together in the modern age in the form of the critic, the thinker, the man who lives between art and the contemplative life—not the intellectual whose job it is to *understand* the whole of reality the way the Platonists hope, but rather by *explaining* reality. And whereas the poet cannot deal with too many events, the critic becomes all events. Reality is only alive to the extent that it can be explained. As with the Platonists and the poets, the word becomes the stamp of truth. An event, or phenomenon, clearly described in a matter-of-fact manner becomes a way of trying to influence reality rather than attain it. Actions and events themselves now become the object of longing, and a clear empirical explanation becomes the process of longing. It leads the critic forward. But again, no single action or event is worth total understanding. Every action, every event, simply becomes another occasion, another attempt for him to banish the feeling of estrangement and fill himself with the 'spirit of kinship.'"

I put down the pages for a while and stared out through the leaded windows. Their thin mullion made a grid of the sky, which seemed like an invitation; it was perfectly clear, a blue plain, a *tabula rasa* (as Locke described the mind), or maybe a *tabula incognita*, on which anything could be written. I lost myself in it for a while. Then a contrail rose above the roofs, chalking a line across the sky. It climbed and disappeared into the top of the window, bisecting the pane, making a door (the door to heaven itself). I watched it thicken and drift, sliding from one side of the frame to the other. I felt an idea stalking inside me, a profound something-or-other, hoping to approach. My phone sounded, issuing its two-tone click. I checked it. It was a news update, a statement from the mayor of New York, saying the campers, squatters, defectors, whatever they were in Central Park, had until the end of the month to disband, pack up and go home. After that, the city would take "whatever action necessary" to remove them. I pulled down and refreshed the page, the throbber spinning, wheeling like one of Aristophanes' hermaphrodites. When I looked up again the sky had changed. The contrail, the door, was gone.

We left the library, heading out into the gathering dark, the cold autumn smell of wet leaves on the breeze. We went to a friend's apartment (we couldn't go back to my place because of Karen, and we couldn't go to Eleanor's because of Jim), a schoolmate's place where we'd been going for weeks on Wednesday evenings. During our session, Eleanor seemed absent, displaced, her deep blackpool eyes roaming some other territory. That old line about the eyes being the window to the soul really was true (I thought about how Goethe believed optics played an active role in the shaping of reality; that is, the sky wasn't simply blue—the interplay between the sky and our eyes *made* it blue). Eleanor's eyes were serious things (when they fixed you, there was nothing you could do) and now they were horizon-wide as she blankly contemplated the ceiling fan, the lamp, the white space above our heads.

"What is it?" I said, on top of her.

"Pull out, please. I have to cough."

Advance Reader Copy

"It's fine."

"I don't want to cough with you inside me."

It was too late. She launched into another fit of rapid contractions and I felt her close up around me, gripping and releasing. It was an odd sensation. When it was over, I placed my head to her chest and eavesdropped on the rattling in her respiratory tract.

"Do you mind?" she said.

I withdrew, waited, then spoke again:

"What is it?"

"I don't know. Don't you find these moments are never what you expect them to be? Every time I'm not here, I want to be here. But when I am here, I'm always somewhere else."

"We're always somewhere else, El."

"But it doesn't make sense. I might wait all day for something like this, and then when it comes… I went to an exhibition with Karen a few days ago—I was looking forward to it all week. And the whole time we were there, I was thinking about other things."

"And it's like that with me?"

"It has nothing to do with you, specifically."

Ironies boiled up in her voice. By contrast, when I spoke with Jim, his voice was full of credulity, a confidence and belief in his level of knowledge about the world he lived in. But Eleanor's was stamped with the sound of doubt.

I got up and made some tea with honey. Eleanor sat on the edge of the bed, naked. I watched her upend the little brown bear and squeeze him into the cup.

"Should we be leaving?" I said. "When's your friend coming back?"

"She's sleeping in the park tonight with a few other people I know. I think I'm going to go down and join them, as soon as I get rid of this cough."

"That's great," I said. "Are you thinking about joining? You know—"

"Yes. If only part-time. I don't think I can be down there every day."

I was excited by this development. Now I had a case study, a real-life example to support my argument that the encampments were the product of some deeper, undiagnosed malaise running through the culture. Eleanor would be my archetype, as she'd always been. I thought of her face again, the one she'd worn when we were having sex, and this, I thought, was the face of my essay. I tried to talk to her about it, but she deflected my attempts.

We got dressed, searching for our clothes on the floor, pulling things out of one another's pant legs. She stood silently, in one sock, in the middle of the room. Even now, she seemed to be looking for something else.

"We should really stop doing this," she said.

Later that night, or earlier the next morning (it was hard to tell when we crossed over), I sat down to work. I had serious business to do. The essay needed to be finished and delivered soon. To date, I had only fragments, notes that I'd taken down in moments of real *frisson*, throbs, fits of inspiration, when the ideas seemed to be coming from somewhere else, beaming into my brain. And the text reflected this: it was a scattershot, miscellaneous bits with no connective tissue. I thought that maybe this could be the form, and I thought about arranging these fragments according to some progression, like Sontag's "Notes on Camp" or Wittgenstein's *Tractatus*, a series of declarative statements, taken as self-evident truths, rather than bothering with a traditional argument.

I sat at my desk, which had a view of the south sky with all its packed vertical irregularities, its hideous glass daggers. Taped around the window were quotes, clippings, things I'd collected over the years. I stuck up a glossy postcard-sized image of *The Death of Marat* that I'd found in one of my books. I didn't admire him at all. He was a bloodthirsty, vulgar pamphleteer. But his influence at the time of the French Revolution demonstrated how writers could be as deadly as armies, turning the *ancien régime* into more than just metaphoric rubble. In its characteristic Romantic style, it was this that the painting sought to immortalize. Following his death, the Cordeliers embalmed Marat's heart and hung it from the ceiling of their assembly, parties adopted him as their official symbol, Montmartre was nicknamed "Montmarat," and after his funeral his body was paraded through the streets of Paris, a torchlit pageant in which people wailed and threw themselves hysterically on the flower-covered coffin.

I worked for a few hours, getting up and down, pacing occasionally, pouring myself a drink. Then I decided to clear out my emails. I'd been neglecting them for weeks—reading them sure, just not responding. I put off all other commitments, even rejecting an invitation to go down to D.C. to speak as part of a panel for a three-day conference on climate change (likely because of the article I'd written on the storm). I ran down the list of speakers: climate scientists, policy analysts, professors of environmental politics. Perhaps they thought they could do with a "literary" perspective for the sake of variety. I respectfully declined. And when they called and offered me a thousand dollars to come down, plus pay my fare and hotel, I declined again. I'd spoken on panels before, but I was far too busy with my current project and couldn't be bothered to think about what I'd said previously regarding the storm. And how would I look up there among the climate scientists and think-tankers, talking about how media events shape our consciousness and constitute our sense of reality? My coevals would be ready with graphs and figures, talking annual measurements in global temperature and cost/benefit analyses, and I'd be up there quoting Wordsworth and talking about the myth of the flood.

I went through my messages. The last one received was from one of my colleagues at the magazine. It said: "Have you seen this?" I ignored it. I didn't need to see it, whatever it was. Then I checked my home page. The internet was exploding over something the president had said the previous evening in Hawaii, while sharing the stage with the Chinese leader, in which he "betrayed the country" by "throwing our intelligence agencies under the bus." I watched the clip (two men in red ties standing in a redwood room flanked with palm trees and flags) and spent the rest of the morning grinding my teeth, as Jim had advised. I posted about it, then posted again, as the cascade of anger came down. I would've rather not, but this couldn't be ignored. We were constantly being called out, or called forth to weigh in on the daily business, to be editors of the moment, and you had to do a certain amount of janitorial work, as Jim liked to say.

But how much time could one devote, even in important, hinge moments, like the one everybody seemed to believe we were living through, to consider all the pain-in-the-ass issues that required your attention: the rising sea levels, the rising murder rates in inner cities, the rising income inequality (and all other risings); refugee crises, political corruption, election interference, government surveillance, famine, plague, poverty, A.I., U.B.I., the still-real threat of nuclear war? I absorbed it all as I did the noise of my fridge or coffee pot, the daily background frequency. None of these events seem to matter much in the grand scheme of things—there were always storms, there had always been abuses of power, corruption, racial injustice, economic inequality; what mattered was that they were happening *now*.

I took my usual perambulatory exercises. Whenever I encountered a block, or couldn't find the energy to compose, I would wander the city for a while, find a patio and take in my surroundings; or I would hop on the subway for a few hours, get off somewhere and walk for a few miles with no destination in mind. I felt I could make a career out of roaming the city. I could spend hours in its architecture, in its elevators, basements, porches, lobbies, staircases and galleries, among the fire escapes, the disharmony of buildings in their Siamese arrangement. The city was a bundle of thoughts, a conscious beehive stacked to the sky, with a million different narratives all vying for space, for recognition.

I needed these intensities. Without them, I lost my perspicacity, my vocabulary seemed to shrink, I was less voluble, my memory for recitation faded. I recalled how I nearly had a panic attack one night while playing pool with Jim at a hotel bar in some bumblefuck town south of the Mason-Dixon. I was unable to remember the word for the table's fabric as the billiard balls slid Newtonianly across its blue-green surface. I went out and circled the block half a dozen times before it finally came to me: *baize*! You couldn't afford this kind of slip of mind in New York. The city wouldn't tolerate you getting so slow. It demanded the very most from you, at all times, and I gave my whole self over to it in return.

I took a few subways around town, packed into trains that sped into hot dark throats, whirling through their circuits like protons inside a giant accelerator. I summoned the layout of the subway map in my mind's eye, the colored tracks racing beneath the concrete, intersecting in their rainbow network. No destination was the point. No guiding purpose or direction. Let yourself bleed in among things, I told myself.

I met Jim in Midtown. He was huddled in front of a shop window, in his dark glasses, his face turned down at a cigarette he was rolling. Cabs crawled through the intersection and engaged in a discourse of horns. Buildings and clouds warped across their windshields.

"About this guy," Jim said.

"Yes?"

"What do we know?"

"Next to nothing," I said. "He's French, that's about it."

"We're not expecting any surprises, are we?"

"Let's hope not. I hate surprises."

"Well, doesn't this whole thing seem just a little fucking shady to you?"

"I know about as much as you at this point. His only contact has been with Bill, and where Bill is currently is just as unknown."

"Why this secrecy?" he said. "Is he on a government watch list?"

"He's on some kind of list. Bill said the French and Spanish governments consider him to be a terrorist. Take that for what it's worth. From what I can tell, he belongs to one of these groups that hang from bridges to prevent oil tankers from leaving port. The kinds of people that get gassed at every G20 summit."

We crossed the street and stopped in front of a blue perimeter fence surrounding a high residential skyscraper. There was the Friedman sculpture standing at the end of the median, towering above the lampposts and traffic lights, a spindly tinfoil man looking up. It seemed like a daily reminder: *Look about you.*

"I've been asked to make an appearance on CNN this week," Jim said.

"What's your slot?"

"Primetime. I'll be in a split screen debate with a senator from Missouri and a journalist from the Post."

"You won't get a word in edgewise."

"I can drop out and recommend you take my place, if you like. I know you've always wanted to be on TV, Paul."

"I'd clam up. I get serious cottonmouth when I know I'm being scrutinized. I'd be on the other side of the screen, chugging water in between points."

In the street, a chimney covering a manhole threw up wreaths of steam that broke and disappeared into the air. It was painted an alternating red and white pattern, like a candy cane. Jim looked around him, doing a witness check. I tried to force him to talk about something else. I was in a slightly melancholy mood and had a mind to reminisce.

"Eleanor was telling me about the time you nearly ran over that kid," I said.

"What kid?"

"Some kid that was in one of her classes. He danced with her at a party or something, and you nearly flattened him in the parking lot."

"She remembers it differently than I do," he said. "What I remember is he kissed her. And I only intended to scare him. Anyway, he didn't strike me as a serious human being."

"I read her thesis. It's quite brilliant," I said.

"I'm sure it is. She's a genius. She's smarter than you and me put together."

My phone vibrated. I checked it.

"Alright," I said.

Jim did one more scan of the area and then we slipped through the perimeter fence. We walked under the huge developing skyscraper, a breezy chicken coop dotted with utility lights. Cranes and hoists hung in orbit around its open top. We made our way across a bed of planks and pulverized earth and Jim made a comment about falling objects. We mounted the staircase which ran up the center of the structure, wrapped around an uncompleted elevator shaft.

"Seventeen," I said.

The street receded as we climbed through the hollow interior. The open cage of trusses and steelwork cut black against the quickening dusk. For a moment I thought that the whole meeting had been a farce, that Jim was secretly leading me up here to confront me and hang me out the window by my lapels with my feet slipping at the edges, like mobsters did in old noir films.

We eventually found our man, sitting on an overturned bucket near a column of rebar. We shook hands and there was a mutual non-verbal recognition, the kind shared by people who have agreed to meet in secret.

"I don't like zis building," he said. "It is, how you say, sore to ze eyes?"

"He speaks English, thank God." Jim said. "For a minute there I thought we were going to have to get somebody up here to translate."

I said, "You know, for someone who doesn't want to draw attention to himself, you certainly picked a difficult place to meet. We could have just gotten in the car and gone back and forth on the highway for an hour or two."

"Non, non. It's like Guy Debord said, Monsieur—you 'ave to subvert ze spaces. Find new expressions, you know. Break into a building and 'ave a congress."

His head reached through the shroud of his hood, pointed, vaguely birdlike, as if all the gravity in him were pulling his face to the end of his nose. His voice was deep, a modulated garble, the freakish timbre one would associate with a thyroid disorder. He was older, in his forties surely, but his manner was adolescent.

"It's a pleasure to meet you, Monsieur Kenning," he said.

"Same."

"I read your piece on ze hurricane you 'ad here. I liked what you say about 'media events shaping ze reality.'"

"Thank you."

"I'm quoting you, *naturellement*. From what I read, I 'sink zat you and I 'ave similar feelings about zese *èvenements*."

"I've wondered what a man in your position wants with someone like me," I said.

"I 'sink you understand what we are trying to do here."

We stood in the frame of a massive window, a large structural square. The blue canvass beat back in the wind, briefly revealing a view of the park.

"I spoke with your editor on ze phone. He was quick to offer your services," he said.

"Bill," I said. "You spoke to Bill."

"So zis Bill sends me to you. I look you up: Paul Kenning. From what I see you are ze kind of man who writes book reviews and 'sink piezes. I wonder what you doing here as well."

Him saying my name in full carried a strange weight, as if he were referring to some past tense version of me, one that already existed in record or memory.

"I have a copy of the pamphlet you and your people published in France," I said. "The writing was for the most part intolerable."

Advance Reader Copy

"I'm not an *homme de lettres*," he said. "I wrote it with my comrades. Of course, I don't 'sink zat you and I disagree much on ze level of ideas. I think we want pretty much ze same things, *non?*"

"I guess we'll find out."

We were losing the daylight. The lamps that populated the lower levels had stopped and now it was only us in steely dark, with the wind working against the tarps and the smell of so much steel it made its way into your mouth.

"How about we start with what you plan to do," Jim said. "The Paris camps you started had no leadership, and no next step. That's why you got broken up. And the same thing will happen here unless you consider what comes after this demonstration."

"You don't 'sink we're talking? I'm 'aving meetings with people here, not just you. We are trying to create a leadership."

"But these movements need to know what their goal is," I said. "What's the object? Why is it happening?"

"You expecting me to explain zis?"

"I was expecting you to explain a few things, yes."

"You want answers. Don't assume I have answers."

"But you agreed to talk to us," I said.

"*Oui.*"

"So you're in a position of authority."

"I'm speaking to you on behalf of ze *événements*. We are looking for publicity in ze U.S.A. Zat is our strategy. You are journalists, no? *Et voila.*"

"But you're in a position to know things," I said. "I mean, you belong to the leadership? You and your group published

Advance Reader Copy

the call to arms, brought all those people out to the climate summit in Paris."

"And we are very proud of zat."

Jim said, "My colleague and I want to publish an open letter and get a bunch of people to sign it."

"We're thinking about doing it," I said.

"And who is going to write it?"

"I am."

"So you're ze filmmaker. And he's ze writer?"

"I like to think of myself as performing the same duty as those writers your country produced in the eighteenth century," I said. "The ones who brought about revolution through paper and ink."

"But zey weren't ze men who stormed ze Bastille, Monsieur. It was people like zat," he said, pointing behind him, toward the park.

"Those writers ennobled the human spirit and made it ripe for transformation!"

"Paul, if you don't mind," Jim said.

"Always you writers talk about zese things. Ze 'uman spirit! Don't talk about zis. Zis is not what ze movement is about."

"Then what is it about?" I demanded.

"We are performing a putsch, Monsieur Kenning. A coup on human attention."

"Yes, but for what?" Jim said. "You've gotten the world's attention. Now you need to think about going after institutions. Developing an agenda. Establishing local groups who can hit the streets and do the legwork."

"You don't consider how big culture changes happen, Monsieur. Zey 'appen slowly. It's not always about ze streets."

"It's about consciousness!" I shouted.

The wind breathed through the quiet colonnade. Below, I saw pairs of white and red taillights sliding down the bright line of Central Park West. The park was a blacked-out space, a monolith.

"For a while we didn't sink beyond ze camps. It started out with a few of us. There was zis summit in Paris, you know— one of zese things where ze politicians, you know, get together and discuss oil prices and emissions and zis shit. So we get together and make zis pamphlet. We publish it online and it went viral. *C'était incroyable.*"

Jim shook his head. He went a few paces in the other direction and then came back, not knowing what to say.

"Maybe you can help me," I said. "I've been asking myself, what do these people want? What do they hope to gain from all this?"

"You can't answer zis, Monsieur Kenning? You are zis great writer, no?

"I have my own ideas, but this isn't about what I think."

"We're getting noticed. Zis is the only language people know now. That's what you said, isn't it, Monsieur: events shape people's sense of ze world? Zey become moments for major changes in consciousness? Monsieur Debord said ze same thing. He called it ze Spectacle. Ze thing zat gets attention is now ze most important form of expression. Zis is what we're doing."

The cherry of his cigarette hovered in the center of his hood, lengthening its glow.

"And what comes of this attention?" I said. "What do you do with it? That's my point."

Jim said, "Listen, what you need to be prepared for is how this thing is going to continue once the camp gets broken up. I got my head beat in a few weeks ago in L.A., and since then the whole effort there has dissolved. If you want this thing to have any life a month from now—a year from now—then you have to be prepared for the end of the occupational part of this movement and to figure out what comes next."

"We're coming to zat realization," he said. "Most of us are non-violent, zough we don't mind some force, of course."

"Are you prepared to do that?" I said. "To let people get their faces smashed?"

"If zat is what it comes to, *quais*."

"I have some contacts in the city," Jim said. "People who are involved with the organization and management of the camps. I can give you their names if you don't already have them."

"And zis open letter?"

"We'll have it ready soon."

"We need to clearly explain what this is about," I said. "It needs to be laid out and people need to sign on to it. Once they understand why, once they think about it—"

"Ze language of ze media isn't thought, Monsieur Kenning. It's crisis. Distraction. Spectacle. Doesn't matter what you say, as long as you get noticed saying it. Ze thing zat matters most

Advance Reader Copy

is ze event zat gets people's attention. Zat is what you wrote about ze storm. Zat's why we are talking, non?"

I was waving my hands, temporarily unable to respond. Jim wandered off and took a piss in a corner and when he came back he tried to wring some kind of coherent agenda out of the man. I listened and felt total disinterest. We exchanged contacts and agreed, conditionally, to meet again, next time with a full group, a party, a congress.

"Can we know your name?" I said.

"It is better if you don't."

He dropped his cigarette on the buffed concrete and stamped it out.

"They'll know someone was here," I said.

"Good," he replied.

We went back down separately, waiting five minutes apart. At the staircase, Jim said:

"This is bullshit. This guy doesn't know anything. It's amazing he and his people got this far."

"I'll write up the open letter tonight," I said. "After that I'm done. You can do whatever you like with him."

Now I was alone, standing in the dark colonnade. I took my time, wandering the floors. I found messages scrawled on the sides of I-beams, little love notes and incoherent graffiti, some of them maybe put there by workers, men who wanted to honor their lovers with immortal tributes stamped on the insides of skyscrapers. I climbed higher until I was looking down on the heads of other buildings. In the distance, I saw the boroughs laid out in light, as I had the night of the storm. I felt lightheaded. I sat on the floor and leaned my head against

Advance Reader Copy

a cold column, receiving vibrations in my skull from the street below. It hummed me to sleep. I hadn't been able to get a full night in a long time. I'd been dozing through my days, catching odds naps here and there. There was an old rumor that DaVinci slept this way so that he could have more time for life. I too disliked being away from life. Dreams were an irrational holiday away from the waking world, what Nabokov called "the nightly betrayal of reason, humanity, genius."

I woke up sometime later, my ass getting cold on the concrete. It was totally dark now. I used the flashlight on my phone to find my way to the staircase. I held the railing all the way down, still feeling dizzy. Maybe there was something wrong with me, or maybe my internal clock had gone out of sync with the clock of Nature (re Leibniz). Or Nature was sending me a signal I needed to take note of: a pang on the inside meant a pang on the outside.

At home I found Karen sitting on the couch in the light of a laptop, fetal position, her large jaw clenched in absent thought, tendons rising in her neck.

On the screen was a video showing twin pillars of black smoke roiling above a desert. It was from some besieged city in Syria, or Yemen, maybe. There were shots of people with bloody faces screaming past a camera with their hands over their heads.

"They're evacuating," she said.

A lonesome helicopter shot swept low through the streets, gliding between the ruined buildings, their facades missing, exposing the stacked three-walled compartments within, bedrooms and kitchens with lamps and chairs idling in dusty sunlight.

She said, "Do you know, I know how to say, 'don't shoot, I'm a journalist,' in twelve different languages?"

There were empty highways scattered with overturned cars, their bellies in the air like toppled insects. We watched people pilfer through the rubble-filled streets and tumbledown masonry—opening shops, smoking in groups, clinging to the old daily tropes, the what-would-be-boredom of a previous life. There were school buses with peaceful white streaks along their sides being led out of the city limits, the faces of evacuated children huddled in the little split windows.

"What's the most danger you've been in?" I said.

"I got roughed up by paramilitary in Egypt a few years ago. They detained me and threw me in jail with a British journalist from *The Guardian*. I was released the next day. He wasn't. I never found out what happened to him."

"Why'd they let you go?"

"They took my camera and destroyed it. I guess after that they had no reason to keep me. I no longer posed a threat. They couldn't remove the words he'd written though. They were already in the airspace, in people's heads."

"They understood the threat."

"What they didn't understand," she said, "is that images are far more dangerous, because they're far more memorable. When people think of Vietnam, they don't think of what was written—they remember that photo of the naked girl running away from a cloud of napalm."

"What was his name—the journalist?" I said, taking out my phone.

"I don't remember. All I know is I got right the hell out of there and took a cab to the American embassy. There were people in the streets burning flags and banging on the windows of our car. Total pandemonium."

The footage rolled on: weeping black-cowled women, keffiyeh-wrapped militiamen, a dog browsing among the brick, smoldering armored units in the sand.

Karen sat up and pulled her knees to her chest, her body collapsed like a lawn chair.

The same stock of clips began to repeat themselves, mingling with live updates, splicing time, such that I could no longer be sure of what had already happened and what was happening currently.

We watched a Russian orchestra perform a concert in the ruins of a liberated city, previously under the control of Islamist militants. It was being held in the bruised remains of an ancient amphitheater that dated back to the days of the Romans. Black coated cellists were arranged in the long Mesopotamian light, sawing away at some melancholy ballad.

"Is it fucked up that I want to be there?" she said.

Karen was addicted to disaster. And she was addicted to the image, the delivery system of disaster. Her claim about being off-duty was only half-true. She still went out during the days, looking for subjects, things to document, and when she returned home, dragging her camera bag along the floor like a miserable kid's march to school, she had the heavy, spent look of having performed a junkie's business. She couldn't keep up. The culture was drunk on the image and demanded it at the rate of lived-life. Like me, Karen belonged to a dying industry, because everyone had her job now. If someone painted their nails or ordered a latte or stood in front of a mirror, there was an image of it somewhere. And if an alien civilization were to visit earth long after our extinction, these would be the artifacts they would uncover and contemplate.

For weeks now we'd been eating dinner together and occasionally I caught her staring at her plate, pausing for a few seconds before finally disturbing the arrangement. And there was the way she would blink after having seen something, making a mental picture, cataloguing the moment, as if to remind herself: *this happened.*

Karen didn't subscribe to the belief, as I did, that some element of our experience was lost in documenting it. For her, images only added to the world. They were *more reality*, and collecting them deepened our experience. I thought that this constituted a new life cycle, based on the acquisition and accumulation of moments that, in sum, let us go to our graves with a sense of having lived. This might have explained why, when Karen found herself alone, with no assignment, she watched the news. She needed to be updated on life, to be reminded that it was still happening, out there.

The next day, I went about sorting—mostly discarding—all the material I'd gathered in the process of composing my essay. Much of it felt used up, spent, drained of whatever meaning it had previously held and now seemed pointless to hang onto. It was cathartic, sweeping the files across my desktop and listening to the crisp sound of them shredding in the trash bin. I stopped to open the "pamphlet," the manifesto that the Frenchman and his people had posted on social media in advance of the Paris climate summit late in the summer, which now felt phenomenally far away to me. Its title page was full of derivative Dadaist imagery: the Botticelli Venus borne forth on the clam, but instead of standing on a clam she stood on a composite skyline that contained famous buildings from various major cities all over the world (the kind of pastiche you sometimes see in the backdrops of nightly news programs), and all around, water was rising up and engulfing the cityscape, while the Venus figure stood there, serene, with scuba gear strapped to her back.

What was the point of this vague, appropriated image? I thought. And what were these people accomplishing, sitting in parks and squares all around the world, waiting? Waiting for what? And what did I care what they did? Yes, the Events lacked consciousness. That was obvious. That was the real problem from the very start. For my part, I had poured my ideas about this into the essay, which, I now realized, contained a nascent criticism of just how hollow and directionless the encampments truly were. In the beginning, I'd wanted to bolster, to instruct. If the culture was in crisis, then it was the role of the critic, as the arbiter of culture, to offer guidance. Now I wanted to expose fallacies. It was no longer about awakening, or awareness, but pointing out the failings of our awareness. This didn't require a rewriting of the essay, per se, only a change in interpretation.

It had been there all along, shouting at me, but in my determination to affirm Hegel's "law of the heart"—the mass flowering of self-consciousness—I'd failed to hear it. So, I decided that I would up my vocalization of the movement's failure. What's more, the camps had become detrimental to their own cause, for aside from being crude, they were already becoming boring, ignorable, contrary to the Frenchman's hope that they were staging a "coup on human attention." And they'd been unable to evolve to the next level, as Jim said. No more would be accomplished with these occupations. There needed to be real organization, mobilization. But I didn't care about that either. The visions I entertained of people marching around the city holding the essay above their heads in affirmation disappeared. Now I wanted to strike a blow, to show everybody just how wrong they were.

At the moment, the Events dominated the news cycle, sure. But it wouldn't last. Narrative is what survives; ideas, words. Yes, soon the park would be vacated, cleaned up, its lawns green and empty again, just as the damage from the flood had

Advance Reader Copy

been cleaned up and the flood itself had receded into memory (and who cared about the flood now? I certainly didn't). But the essay, that *would* survive. And I remained confident, despite this change in attitude, that its argument was still one hundred percent true, perhaps even more now than ever.

I spent most of the morning thinking about this, mooning in my lavish bath. I lay submerged, my frame canted along the length of the tub, hearing the distant heaving wails of police sirens below. The townhouses over the park turned a hushed gold, their amalgam of concrete and glass all ringing with this new clarity. I kept running through the argument in my head. Yes, yes, I said, agreeing with myself. It was almost ready to go. It was almost true and good and right. And it was everything else that was confused.

El and I met again for our uptown tryst. Our sex had become disconnected. There was no spirit, none of the usual quest and curiosity. In her texts she'd sounded earnest and appealing, but now she seemed totally deflated. She barely spoke. I watched her stomach rise and fall in the sidelong light. She went in and out of sleep and I picked blades of grass out of her hair. She'd been living in the park part-time with some friends. Again, I tried to ask her why she was interested in the Events and why she felt it necessary to join them, but she ignored me, changing the subject. We scrolled the feed together, with Eleanor holding her device up over our heads, changing hands occasionally. We rolled past new stories, pictures of people's pets, dream vacation destination photos, makeup tutorials and an informational video about palm oil showing a flattened jungle terrain, a lopped colonnade, orangutans stranded in the treetops; a viral video from some late-night comedian who had "eviscerated" the president on their show the previous evening; then a tour of the latest book reviews, with quick sallies into podcast clips and pictures of girls (Eleanor's friends) posing in front of their mirrors at home, or in their office bathrooms, and interspersed throughout all of these were memes, screenshots, random quotes, mostly from writers and public intellectuals, excerpted from texts new and old, bits of criticism, wisdom, inspiration, ideas people were supposed to heed and remember. Eleanor opened one of these pages and found that whoever was curating this content had included something I'd written. The text was laid overtop my face. I almost didn't recognize it; it seemed to have been written by somebody else. Eleanor took a shower, disappearing for a bit. I lay in bed, contemplating the white ceiling, the dead, negative space. I felt stretched, extended, my nerves humming. Then my phone clicked. I opened my eyes. It may as well have been a tap on the window. The world was once again calling us outside. Eleanor came from the bathroom and collapsed on top of me like a wet sandbag. I traced words into her back with my finger and asked her what I was spelling out. After a while she fell asleep again, snoring loudly, while I ran through the essay in my head and wrote it out across her body.

Bill Morning called some hours later. I sat up in the dark. The curtains were drawn. The blue light of my phone flashed against the ceiling, reestablishing the room's dimensions.

"Hello? Do I have the right number?"

"That depends on who you're looking for," I said.

"You mean this isn't Pearly Gates Crematorium? *You die, we fry.*" Bill's laugh was aged, cut with phlegm and bile built up over decades, like your grandfather's laugh. "I've been waiting for weeks to squeeze that one out," he said.

"You sound like you're in a good mood, Bill."

"I don't know why I'm making jokes. I feel awful actually."

I expected him to sound robust, but he was weak and husky, a sharp departure from last time. The minerals he was imbibing were abrading him from the inside out.

I got up and pulled back the shades.

He said, "Is it dark where you are?"

"Nearly. I'm wandering around the house, watching the sun set over the park."

"The buildings bleeding into each other."

"Yes."

"And that little red flare that comes over New Jersey and mingles with the smokestacks."

"Yeah, just like that."

"I can see it now. The mental picture is perfect. I miss it. I'm at a hotel with Elsa. We're somewhere in the southern hemisphere. I feel upside down. All the stars are different here."

I heard him groan as if he were settling himself in a chair. I did the same.

"How are the camps?" he said.

"You know," I said. "Same as they were before. 10,000 people and nothing happening. The city refuses to call it a commune."

"Why?"

"I think they feel that calling it a commune would confer power upon it—make it seem like a legitimate entity. They're sticking to 'lawful assembly.' But your man who spoke to us a few nights ago gave us the impression that it won't stay peaceful for too much longer."

"Right, how did that go?" he said.

"We talked for an hour or so. It's funny, he insists we have a lot in common, despite certain profound disagreements."

"Such as?"

"Well, he believes that the events are fundamentally a media spectacle, designed to disturb people's complacency," I said.

"And you agree with him?"

"Maybe, but we have different conclusions."

"That's essentially what you said in your piece about the storm: that the culture of events has become the new narrative—it forms our *weltanschauung*, or whatever term you used. You used a German word, I know that. You seem to like German words, Paul."

"Please don't quote me back to myself, Bill. Jesus, if there's one thing I can't take today, it's that."

"There's something to it," he said. "Lately, I've been thinking about the news I really remember from my life—what I've seen, what I've lived through. The mind tends to look backward at this stage, you know."

"And?"

"It's mostly death and tragedy. I was thinking about the day Lennon was shot. It happened three blocks from my building. Everybody in the city was friends that day. People were quiet everywhere I went. There was less honking in the streets. Every bar in the city was playing The Beatles. The rest of the world seemed to be put on hold. I got more phone calls that day than when my dad died."

"What I said, Bill, was that we focus ourselves around these events, locate ourselves within them. The medium has become mingled with the mind, and the event that focuses the medium focuses the mind by extension."

"Yes, well said."

"I'm sending Carol the essay tomorrow or the next day," I said. "You should be able to read it sometime next week."

"Looking forward. I'll watch the magazine racks at the airport and let you know if I see people reading it."

"Remember the looks on their faces and report back to me."

He withdrew the receiver and coughed.

"Where are you now?" I said.

"Not sure. Elsa has control of our travel plans. She stays up all night on the internet, booking flights and reading about shamans and miracle workers in remote corners of the globe."

"Why did you call, Bill? Just to know how the sun was setting?"

"I'm dying, Paul."

"I know."

"And you know, for some reason, I feel good talking about it with you. I liked what you said in one of your pieces—about how 'ideas are our revenge on the world for having to die.' I've been reading your work again, as you can tell."

"You've always been my biggest champion, Bill."

"I'm starved for dialogue, Paul. I haven't had a decent conversation in a month, and I'd like to have one that doesn't involve documents or wills or pensions or anything *post mortem*."

"I don't see what I can tell you that will be of any help. I'm thirty-three, Bill. What do I know about sickness and death? You should be talking with people who have been where you are."

"Those people are dead. Besides, I can't really talk to anyone anymore. When you become ill, it's like a group of men come into your home and sweep you off to another realm; you cross the threshold of the land of the living and enter the land of the sick, where you can only communicate through a glass wall with a phone, like in prison. That's the worst part about it. You know how the only thing you can talk about with your co-workers is work? Or how famous people are only friends with other famous people? It's because they belong to an alien society and they can only relate to each other. And I don't have any dying friends."

"But you feel good calling me? Well, I'm happy to help in any way I can, Bill."

"I try to talk about it with Elsa, but it's like trying to persuade a horse to cross a river. She's skittish as hell."

"Can you blame her?"

"No. But she's still invested in the idea that these holistic remedies are doing something for me. She doesn't want to acknowledge—"

"That, yeah. Yeah, I get you."

There was a bit of static coming through the signal, atmospheric noise, clutter.

"So where are you at?" I asked.

"Time-wise? Or stage-wise?"

"Both."

"Well, the cancer has metastasized to my lymph nodes," he said. "You know I've always liked that word, *metastasized*. Doctors love to say it too. They always pronounce it fully, eloquently, emphasizing all the syllables. Too bad it denotes such an ugly thing."

"Yeah, too bad. Fuck."

"But now that I'm not burdened by anxiety about the future, the outcome is much simpler. The simpler things become, the simpler the joys are. I've been crying at faces in the street, welling up at the prospect of a beer."

"I hear people say things like that a lot," I said.

"Sex has also improved considerably."

He coughed again, deep and rocky. He sounded as if he were calling up his whole being and sending his innards through the line. For a moment I caught the surrounding noise of trees and wind and traffic, of wherever he was. He settled himself again.

He said, "You know, there was a time when I would have said that the worst part about dying would be the day the papers came out and I wouldn't be there to read them."

Outside, beyond the glass, objects and surfaces slowly came into focus as my eyes adjusted to the light. My mind was awake, but my visual field was still coming online.

"Anyway, I feel like you've always understood the terms," he said. "Writers are always trying to have the last word on life. Some nights I used to go to bed after finishing an article and think 'if I die tomorrow that would be okay, now that I've said my piece.'"

"I always feel like, 'I just have to stay alive long enough to finish this thing.' This essay has had me in a death grip for the last month."

"Does it make you angry?"

"I'm getting angry just sitting here talking about it," I said.

"I can't manage that. It seems like wasted energy. I always thought I wouldn't be at the party as long as everyone else. I just expected to leave on my own terms."

"Leave behind a body of ideas. That's what's important. A *corpus*. The language of death is written into our jobs."

"I have a lot of ideas about what's ahead of me, none of which are the least bit comforting," he said. "But I can't muster the hope or despair necessary to believe in them." He paused, presumably to collect himself. "I think it's people," he continued. "People are what redeem death. I think believing in other people's aliveness is what makes life worth living; and not just viewing them as objects around your own consciousness. That's what's important to me. Maybe that's why I called to talk."

At this I was silent. I suddenly found I didn't have anything to say.

"You know, a few years ago Elsa and I were in Mexico City for the Day of the Dead. The whole city practically shut down. There were people dancing in the streets, torch lit parades, big bands, kids running around in skull masks. There's a culture that understands how to treat death—put it out there in the streets, dress it up, make a festival of it. When my time comes, make a spectacle of me, light me up on the six o'clock news. Speaking of which, I've made some calls to the people at NASA. I asked if they'd be willing to take my ashes up as cargo during one of their satellite launches. They think they can do it—for a price. It costs about ten thousand dollars to send a pound of anything into space. You could send a pound of shit up there and it would be the most expensive shit in the world."

"Well, spaces launches are all the rage these days," I said. "Elon Musk will send you up on a live stream."

The call dropped and the line went dead. I sat there for a few moments, holding the screen against the shell of my ear. This talk of death had obliterated my eloquence. Bill was looking for someone to speak to and I was unable to provide even a quote with which to console him. And what would I have to say on the subject anyway? While Bill was facing down

Advance Reader Copy

the fact of non-existence, I was worrying about not accomplishing anything before non-existence. He was worried about death and I was worried about lack-of-relevance. I was still firmly in the business of life, acquisition, experience, knowledge, producing the necessary materials to keep death a far-off issue. I still had reason to read the news, write, and so on. But what did it matter to Bill now if the Earth was warming at an exponential rate, if human civilization was unsustainable—if the Events had been a huge failure? The news didn't matter when you were dead.

With this in mind, I suddenly wanted to talk more. I tried to call the number back but got no answer. There was only silence at the other end of the line. There was something in the transmission, the way he sounded right before he signed off, something in the chambered, disembodied voice being relayed to me through the small slat at the top of my phone—as if it were coming from another territory altogether—that seemed to affirm this one unshakeable fact: this would be the last time I would ever speak to Bill Morning.

I continued my conversations with Jim. We walked against the falling November light, the hour of sunflares and quivering shades, which were so conducive to contemplation.

But these days our talks were scattered and cut with silences—a comment about Jim's annual libidinal remission sweeping into his newfound wealth, his film and the collapse of his love life (he spoke about a period of "desexualization," like the deStalinization of the Soviet Union in the fifties). The language of politics was appropriate: Jim's domestic failures had driven him to activism and social justice, and he was exchanging the quiet struggles of personal life for the worldly struggles of public life. The boundaries between these sectors had blurred in the wake of the Events; now his relationship was in shambles, Eleanor was living in the camp, and Jim was at the height of his moral duties as a celebrity with a conscience. With this I could sympathize. At the moment, I had a three-body problem I couldn't solve; a woman I barely knew was sharing my bed and clipping her toenails in my toilet, and here I was, out strolling the park, trying to keep up with the culture.

Jim didn't say much. He seemed to be bracing himself for something. He wasn't delivering his usual agitated monologues, but walking quietly beside me, the late light on his handsome and still-bruised face as we took a path under a vault of Japanese trees. The Events were a frequent topic, of course, but I had little interest in engaging him when it came to this. I didn't bother to report to him how my feelings on the matter had changed, in order to spare myself the cannonade of shit I would doubtlessly endure.

I'd also decided not to write the open letter. Instead, Jim would release a short video in which various celebrities and public intellectuals expressed their support for the camps. I told him this was the better move. Every day it seemed some new famous face came to the park to make a speech, have their picture taken, or sleep overnight to illustrate their solidarity. The attention of celebrities conferred a vogue status on the movement. People would be wearing colored ribbons soon, and whoever won best actor at the Academy Awards next year would reserve time in their acceptance speech to acknowledge the Events.

We drifted to Jim's office uptown. He hadn't spoken a word since getting on the subway. He went about the room, switching things on, grabbing boxes and moving them around absently. The walls were covered with lists and schedules and to-dos, a map of the island with an area marked out in its center where the camp was located, circled in red.

"I want to show you something," he said.

We sat down at his computer. He clicked through a tree of files and pulled up a video. He pressed play and there appeared the face and body of Eleanor Blue, sitting on a windowsill with a look of prearranged boredom. It was in their apartment, somewhere near evening. She was watching Jim set up, coming in and out of focus, her eyes following the lens as it roamed back and forth. Jim had done many screen tests like this during pre-production for his film. He wanted Eleanor in front of the camera. He needed to see her like this.

JIM: "Tell us your name, please."
ELEANOR: "Eleanor Blue. Wait, I forgot my middle name."
JIM: "That's fine. Why don't you sit down?"
ELEANOR: "I'll sit here."

JIM: "Having the window open like that is going to mess with the sound."

ELEANOR: "I'm fine here."

Eleanor sucked on yellow lozenge. A cough drop. She held it between her teeth whenever Jim spoke.

JIM: "Where are you from?"

ELEANOR: "You know."

JIM: "And how old are you?"

ELEANOR: "Twenty-six."

JIM: "What do you study?"

ELEANOR: "I study literature and philosophy. At the moment I'm getting my PhD, writing about Western love poetry."

JIM: "Would you rather have a cellphone or a PhD?"

ELEANOR: "Can't I have both?"

JIM: "You know your phone contains coltan metal, which is mined in places like the Congo with what is essentially slave labor? And then assembled in factories in China where people hurl themselves out windows because the conditions are so terrible?"

ELEANOR: "I'm aware of this."

JIM: "Are you?"

ELEANOR: "I read the news, yes. I'm reminded every day of what a terrible person I am."

JIM: "If you had to choose between your cellphone and the Earth's climate returning to a manageable stasis, what would you choose?"

ELEANOR: "What is the point of this?"

JIM: "I just want you talking. I'm getting my levels."

ELEANOR: "You're getting more than that."

JIM: "Do you believe the American government is a force for good in the world?"

ELEANOR: "When it behaves itself, yes."

JIM: "And these Events—do you believe they are a force for good?"

ELEANOR: "Maybe."

JIM: "And do you think they have a future?"

Before she could answer Jim came into frame and adjusted the microphone on her shirt. "You know, it might be easier if you just clip it," he said. "Here—pull your hair back, it's rubbing up against it. And spit that thing out." He went back behind the camera. There was a silence. Then I heard his zippo clasp shut.

JIM: "So, what do you want to start with?"

ELEANOR: "What, you don't want to chat first—shoot the breeze?"

JIM: "Let's start, as a wise man once said, not with the good old things, but the bad new things."

ELEANOR: "I figured you wanted to revisit old quarrels."

JIM: "I feel bad about things, and I want you to have this opportunity to say whatever you want to say."

ELEANOR: "I'm in a generous mood. You might get everything."

JIM: "I want you to speak. We don't speak anymore."

ELEANOR: "You want to have a real talk?"

JIM: "A real talk."

ELEANOR: "While you point that thing at my face and interrogate me?"

There was a beat. Jim was thinking. I imagined he looked as he did now, sitting next to me with his steepled fingers under his nose.

JIM: "Why don't we begin with why you've decided to start living in the park."

ELEANOR: "Let the overeducated kid prattle on? I don't want to prattle."

JIM: "Prattle. Rant. Embarrass yourself by having an opinion. I don't care."

ELEANOR: "The world already knows my opinions. You put them up on the screen for everybody to see."

JIM: "This isn't about that though. This is about us. Don't worry about how you're going to appear."

ELEANOR: "I can't not."

JIM: "And why is that?"

ELEANOR: "Because nothing hides now. Everything is broadcast—every experience, every whim and half-formed thought has to be put out there. Nothing exists until it's recorded. Consider what we're doing now."

JIM: "And this makes you afraid to express your opinion?"

ELEANOR: "In so far as every opinion is a liability, yes."

JIM: "What do you care more about? Truth, or opinion?"

ELEANOR: "You don't have enough film for that."

JIM: "But aren't we suffering from a kind of intellectual inflation? Hasn't the abundance of opinion diminished the value of truth in the culture?"

ELEANOR: "You sound like Paul."

JIM: "But you understand."

ELEANOR: "Of course! I don't know if I can say that I really *know* anything. All I have is information and the opinions of others. I'm stuck in the cave."

She stopped at a high breeze, pulling strands of hair back from her face. There was a lull and she looked away at the sound of something in the street.

ELEANOR: "In about ten minutes that light is going to be in my eyes."

JIM: "Don't lean."

ELEANOR: "Don't lean."

JIM: "Well, I want your opinion. You can't tell me why you've decided to pack up and start living in a tent in the middle of Central Park? I mean, you must have a reason."

ELEANOR: "We all have our reasons. I don't think anyone actually knows why they're part of this thing. Or what it signifies. No one talks about it. I haven't heard that much about politics since I've been down there. People mostly just share their stories."

JIM: "Everyone's got a fuckin' story, jeez."

ELEANOR: "I honestly can't tell you why."

JIM: "There are the obvious causes though."

ELEANOR: "I think I'm too young to have causes. Causes are for people who have lived through things and want to improve conditions for younger generations. People talk about leaving a better world for their kids and I still consider myself one of those kids. Let other people have causes."

JIM: "I won't accept that as an answer."

ELEANOR: "Well, you're going to have to. Unless you want to make another movie about it. I'm not a thing to be understood, Jim. You and Paul are two of a kind. You both place so much importance on having to *understand* things, so that you can contain them and manage them. For years now, I've been studying how people have tried—for centuries—to explain things, and have failed. I've been trying to explain it myself— to explain the explainers—and now I'm sick of explanations. Maybe that's why I've started sleeping on the Great Lawn with ten-thousand other people."

She spoke softly and with managed intensity, as if she had been rehearsing these words in her head for years.

ELEANOR: "It always had to be something bigger than me. I wasn't enough by myself. You had to make some goddamn grand narrative of it."

On the monitor I watched Eleanor's gaze settle, silent and affirming, those heavy blackpool eyes. It was a look that stepped out of some long-held weariness and anxiety. She looked straight through the lens at both of us.

JIM: "Does loyalty mean anything to you?"

ELEANOR: "I don't think either of us are in any position to be discussing loyalty. We failed. We both failed. Let's just leave it at that. We don't need to explain it, Christ. And we certainly don't need to document it."

She got up and walked out of frame. For a moment I half-expected her to enter the room where we were sitting.

JIM: "We're not done yet."

ELEANOR: "We were done a long time ago, James."

JIM: "What do you do in the evenings after you leave the library?"

ELEANOR: "You want to know? I suppose it's about time."

JIM: "I want you to tell me everything."

ELEANOR: "How many minutes do you have?"

JIM: "As many as I need."

"I don't need to see any more of this," I said, standing.

Jim closed random files and stared at the screen, not acknowledging me.

"It goes on like that," he said. "I have about six hours of it. It was productive. She told me things."

I studied the silence and thought it was better to speak first.

"I'll tell you everything you want to know," I said. "How long, when, and where it happened."

"There is nothing you can say."

"I feel like I owe you."

"You don't owe me shit."

"We can be decent humans about this, Jim."

"Fuck you, decent humans."

"You owe me, and I owe you."

"I could bash your goddamn head in," he said. "How about that?"

He struck me in the ear with his phone, the closest throwable object. This was a preface, an introductory strike. He got up and stood for a moment to consider his next move. Then he grabbed my phone and loaded it behind his back like he was preparing to toss a discus.

"Jim."

The device flew past my head and lodged itself in the drywall. It awoke from its sleep, responding to the motion. The toss activated the camera and turned the flash on.

· 155 ·

"She told me everything, Paul. She's incapable of keeping a secret. She's too honest. She even managed to do it in a way that seemed like she was being the better person for telling me. She somehow left with the high ground."

"I should tell you that it's Platonic," I said.

"So the two of you get together and talk?"

"In a way."

"Jesus Christ."

"I really am quite fond of her, Jim."

"Watch what you say. I'm considering giving you a pass here."

"Would it help if I told you that it was my fault—that I convinced her to do it?"

"Your stories would be out of sync then. She told me she did it not to get back at me, but because she needed something for herself, something private, unknown to the world."

"Makes sense."

"Funny thing is, if it was going to happen, I'm glad it happened with you. And not some random person."

He took a few steps and braced himself on the radiator. He sat for a moment with his head back against the wall. He seemed dizzy, still feeling the residual effects of his concussion, but it was difficult to tell. His expression was concealed beneath his dark glasses.

"I've known for months," he said. "She didn't have to tell me. I left my phone in the drawer with the recorder running one evening while you two were fooling around."

"You never said."

"I wanted to hear it. From her." The bruise above his left eye had yellowed, a blot smeared with purple and blue. "Women." He laughed.

"We were always pretty much in agreement on that subject."

"Don't do that."

"What?"

"That. Be all chummy just because I won't kill you."

"I've accepted whatever's coming to me," I said. "I probably deserve it."

I settled my hands on the chair in front of me and leaned into it for support. I watched him. His face was down and his hands were in his pockets.

"We used to agree on a lot more," I said.

"We never agreed on anything."

"We used to spend hours on the curb outside the bar before either one of us could get into a cab. We argued in the bar and then we argued outside."

"We'd call cabs, and they'd leave us."

"You came with me all the way to Queens once just to make your point about something I can't even remember now."

He lowered his eyes. I went to the wall and dislodged my phone. Then I picked his up off the floor and placed it on the table in front of us, still not wanting to get close to him, not sure if he wanted me to.

I said, "You know she felt awful about it. It was nothing malicious, nothing sinister. I really am fond of her, Jim."

"You already said that."

"I'll let you decide what you want to do. I'm ready for it."

"I'm not going to do anything," he said. "We understand each other now, that's all.

My ear was warm, glowing with pain.

"I've heard that affairs can actually strengthen a relationship," I said. "It might be productive to think of this as a stress test on the way to something more earnest and meaningful."

"Fuck you, Paul. You don't get to talk to me like that."

"Look, I don't want any of this hanging over us. I think it's important that we have dialogue—really hash it out, so there's no lingering resentment."

"El and I have made our plans. That's all that matters."

"So things are…?"

"We've reached a tentative agreement, which seems to be the best thing for us right now."

"Would it be in poor taste to ask what that is?"

"I won't be making a film about this one, I can tell you that."

"So things are?"

"I'm sure she'll tell you."

He was quiet for a while. I stayed put and went through the requisite motions of nuanced analysis as he cleaned up. The sun fell on his head, illuminating the track of staples that ran through his black, matted hair. I went to the bathroom and ran cool water over a paper towel and held it to the cut that had been made along my ear. When I came back, he was sitting there, answering his emails, checking his newsfeed, calm, unmoved, as if nothing at all had taken place just now. After a few minutes, I came and sat down next to him, absently folding the wet towel in my hands.

"I read your essay," he said. "It's supposed to go up tomorrow?

"Yes," I said.

There was a silence.

"You want to know what I think about it?" he said.

"I do."

"It's exactly the kind of thing I expected you to write," he smiled. "That's all I'll say."

This was a sign that he was in an improving mood. We sat there together, me on my phone and he on his computer, engaged in our separate tasks, reading, not speaking to one another. An article came up about the camps in San Francisco and I didn't even bother to check it. I was bored, feeling little to none of the intensity that I had at times over these past few weeks. It all seemed like wasted matter, something that would be half-remembered, yet another world event bound for nowhere. After an hour or so, I got up and left without saying a word.

The next day I opened my emails to find that Bill Morning had died. The news came from his wife Elsa. It was a mass message, delivered to some several hundred recipients. It was terse, with some regrettable stock phrasing that made me cringe: "It is with a heavy heart that I inform you that my husband, your friend and colleague, Bill Morning, passed away yesterday due to complications related to treatment of his cancer." This was curious. What complications, I thought? What treatment? Then it struck me that it most likely involved the copious amount of volcanic rock he'd been ingesting over these last few weeks. The zeolites had hollowed him out. I checked the time. The email had been sent in the middle of the night, which meant they were likely in another time zone (a day ahead, a day behind?) The timing suggested that Bill must have died within twenty-four hours after I'd last spoken to him. It was possible, I thought, that he died immediately following our call. Maybe that's why he said he didn't feel well and hung up.

I was unshocked by the news. In some ways, he was dead on the day he told me about his illness(es), because he'd already been pronounced dead: his name was in the database, the bank of obituaries, waiting for its release. He was dead when I read his letter of resignation in the magazine, and a few weeks later when I met with him for the last time, at LaGuardia. The email went on to say that there would be no funeral service, and I knew the reason why: Bill was going to realize his dream of being launched into low Earth orbit. One of the tech billionaires would fire him into space, along with a couple other celebrities. He was going to have his ashes scattered in the atmosphere; he would become part of the air traffic, the space junk, just another thing up there that navigators would have to dodge. I'd look for him in the coming months, rocketing over the building tops.

Not knowing what to say, I wrote down Macbeth's lines, the ones he delivers after the murder of the king, and sent them to Elsa:

Better be with the dead
Whom we, to gain our peace, have sent to peace,
Than on the torture of the mind to lie
In restless ecstasy. Duncan is in his grave;
After life's fitful fever he sleeps well.

It was fitting that the news of Bill's death had been delivered in writing—the written word being the only real shot at immortality we have. Every time I sat down, I thought about how this sentence, or that paragraph would be received a hundred years hence—how the words fly through time and land in the heads of future strangers. The truth was that all writers belonged to a cult of death because we all sought posterity.

What is it like to enter into the culture? Not just as a noun, an entry in the dictionary, but as a thing, an item, a page, a piece of information in some database. If you're lucky enough to be remembered, you have the chance to live again every time someone searches you—because you're part of the signal, the feed. You become a fact, an event. Now Bill's death had become one of these events, another thing added to the world, within the world, an errant article roaming the airspace, waiting to be called up, read about, consumed. I thought of my essay in the same vein. Today it was going "live." I liked the word—*Live*. It too would take on its own being, become a living thing. It would go out and mingle with people's minds, becoming part of their consciousness. For weeks it had been a secret, private knowledge I had only with myself. Now it belonged to everyone.

Though I'd spent weeks laboring over it, the essay was fairly short, and that was the point. It was intended to have intensity, clarity, and candor. It was meant to be, in a word, *perfect*. Every sentence was to be a great sentence, each statement a truth, a cloud-parting insight. And yet, it had failed to deliver the feeling of confirmation I'd anticipated upon finishing it. But it was still too early. I was waiting, poised for the reaction, the response, the hails of virtual applause and agreement, the "amens" and "finally!"s and "yes, yes, yes"s. Or, the violent objections, the accusations of "blindness," or "deafness," or whatever, the vitriol, the willful misreadings and misinterpretations.

I'd also expected the essay to change the appearance of things slightly, or at least my perspective. I recalled an anecdote, probably apocryphal, about how Rutherford, on the day after he discovered that atoms were composed mostly of empty space, was afraid to climb out of his bed for fear he would fall through the floor. This was the awful knowledge he shared with himself before releasing it into the minds of others. I'd half-expected, in an elevated mood, to have a similar experience, to step onto a different floor that morning.

I brooded on these questions for a few hours, checking my feed regularly, and then went out into the mild pre-winter afternoon. I took the train downtown and came up into the red and brown brick streets of the meatpacking district. Last time I was here, I was ankle-deep in riverwater. The cobble streets led me once again to the High Line, where once again the Frenchman was waiting for me.

"We are 'aving good luck, Monsieur," he said. "It's last day of November and we still in ze fifties. It's fifties, right? I know centigrade. If I wasn't atheist, I'd say god was blessing our little movement."

"We're not lucky," I said, slightly annoyed. "The Earth is heating up at an accelerating rate, and with the way things are going, this whole city will be under water in a hundred years. Isn't that why you're protesting?"

"Is zis what you want to make today's conversation about?"

"I already published my piece. I'm done."

"Zis is a friendly visit, Monsieur Kenning. I can see now zat you and I disagree about ze *événements*, but I wanted to meet again because I feel our last talk was productive, no? I'm also looking to make some American comrades while I'm here."

"Well now that we're comrades, I suppose it wouldn't do you any harm to tell me your name."

Advance Reader Copy

"Jean."

"I expected something like that."

"And you're Paul. Ze first theologian. Ze first explainer!"

He was in a t-shirt this time. He looked like a Marfan child, long and stooped, full of pockets and hollows, his head was shaved and his bug-like eyes orbited in their deep sockets. We walked along the promenade, the sounds of the street wafting up to us, the smokebush and milkweed plants dying in the overgrowth between the bright rails.

"I'm surprised you're not at the park," I said. "Aren't you needed?"

"I'm connected to ze camp's main network," he said, patting the bulge his phone made in his pocket. "I keep up to date on ze daily activities. I don't need to be zere all ze time."

"Who runs the network?"

"People way smarter than you and I, Monsieur. You see, even camping in ze park relies on technology now, eh?"

"Do you want a drink, Jean? I could go for a drink."

"Should I tell you we've got some plans for zis weekend?"

"I don't know, should you?"

"We going to make a final demonstration. We are not announcing it. Zis is going to be spontaneous. We going to march through ze streets, across bridges, walk into ze buildings, take elevators up to offices, disrupt everything. Shut ze city down."

"That can only end badly."

"We going to try to get into ze stock exchange as well."

"Is Jim involved in this?"

"*Non.* In fact, your friend has been quite, how you say—stubborn about ze whole thing? We had a meeting last week. About twenty of people. We had a big fight."

"He doesn't think much of your philosophy,' I said.

It was the noon hour and people were lunching under glass canopies. The biergarten buzzed below us, taxis hummed near curbs, the ventilation units belched and droned. The sun, high over the Hudson, made the river into a mirror. Jean paused while he checked his phone, still walking as we came upon the industrial exterior of the Whitney.

"Will you participate?" he said.

"I'm a man of ideas, Jean. I build my days around phrases, trying to reach the bottom of the page before I go mental. I've already made my contribution. Or do you really need me with a Molotov cocktail in my hand?"

"I don't sink you've considered how you might feel tipping over a car or throwing a brick through a window."

"I'm a pacifist," I said. "A militant pacifist."

We reached the stairs of the museum and climbed the cantilevered steps to the roof. Jean stared ahead, his hands out, containing something in the air in front of him.

He said, "I've wondered, why does a man like you care about what happens with zis movement? You obviously 'ave no interest in our goals. And yet you agreed to meet with me."

"I still don't know what your goals are. That's part of your problem."

"But why do you feel zis obligation?"

"What was Sartre's obligation to the resistance?" I said. "Or Zola's to Alfred Dreyfus? Or Orwell's to the Spanish Civil

Advance Reader Copy

War? Writers have an obligation to support or oppose shifts in the culture. It's our duty. I consider myself to be a part of the same tradition, though I have no interest in going to war, and don't hunger for violence the way someone like Sartre did. But I understand the responsibility."

"So zis is about responsibility then?"

"Yes."

"But a piece of writing no longer has ze power to instruct, no? To *ennoble*, as you say? Only demonstrations like ours can do zat now. There's too much noise. How else can you get above it? Zat's why we are here, Monsieur Kenning. Because criticizing ze culture isn't enough anymore. You express dissent one day, and your culture absorbs it and spits it back at you ze next."

"You asked me what I believe, Jean. That's what I believe."

"Our beliefs are more—how you say, *compatible*—zan you sink. We both 'ave our enemies, our targets. We both hate ze same things, want to see ze same changes. We're in ze same business. Difference is you use words. I use bodies in ze streets."

We reached the rooftop. Jean was visibly out of breath. A group of young Canadian girls approached me and asked if I'd take a picture of them against the balustrade, with Lena Halley's building in the background.

"You know," I said, "Conrad believed that in order to understand any event, to see the full scope of a human experience, we needed words."

"People don't know Conrad, Monsieur. What zey know are events. What do zey teach you Americans in school: Hiroshima? Ze moon landing? Ze Civil War? Every school kid knows zese things. It's events that make history."

"Facts, facts, facts," I said. "That's all people know. Can you name all forty-five presidents? Who discovered electricity? Never mind telling us anything about it, just the year it happened."

"*Exactement*. See, we're both critics. You use laptop, I use thousands of people."

"All those people," I said. "I have to admit, I never thought it'd last this long. These things have a way of dying out after a few weeks. I admire their persistence."

"It's a sign zat we're not going away. People won't be able to feed zeir cats without sinking about us."

"I detest crowds, Jean. I've participated in a few protests in my time, and I could never summon the passion to adopt the slogans, chant along, make the posters, stomp my feet. I even avoid sporting events because I hate the atmosphere of thousands of people all thinking the same way so close together."

"I'm not surprised to hear zis misanthrope talk, Monsieur. Most people in your line of work are misanthropes, non?"

"Jim is the same way," I said. "For a 'man of the people' he can be remarkably mean. He seems to have a special contempt for people in the service industry."

"But I'm sure you've heard zis before."

"Yeah, yeah."

Jean leaned against the balustrade, taking quick draws off a cigarette that was pinched rodentially between his lips. The breeze on top of the museum was nice. It was warm enough to take off your jacket. I was actually enjoying myself.

"Demonstrations are beautiful things," he said. "They are statements made with ze body. You take your body outdoors and put it in ze streets where it will be seen. If enough people do zis, then you have ze power."

"The individual will versus the collective will," I said.

"I'm sure I know your feelings on zat."

"Writers are fierce individualists. The hive mind is our enemy."

"But you're just like zem, non? You're miserable and want your misery to be acknowledged by ze rest of ze world? Zere's little difference between you and all zose people sleeping on ze grass."

"Not exactly an intelligent commentary."

"You're looking for understanding, Paul."

"I understand," I said. "And now I need to go."

"Zis was supposed to be a friendly chat. We barely started."

"We'll do it again sometime."

"We are like zose two men in ze movie, Casablanca?"

"I'll drop in on you next time I'm in Paris."

"Keep in touch, Paul Kenning. I may need something from you in ze future."

"Jean, I think this is the start of a terrible friendship."

Eleanor had been living in the park pretty much full time for the past few weeks, going home periodically only to shower and grab clean underwear. If the purpose of the camps really was to give a human face to some abstract alienation, disaffection, malaise, as I'd contended, then when I tried to summon what this face might look like, I could only picture lovely, sad, tragic, Eleanor Blue. I was being disingenuous in not admitting to myself that the real reason I was still making daily visits to the camps was to be with her. I wanted to give myself over to this woman, totally. I wanted to come home and crawl up next to her, join our two halves, legs entangled, take her into my hands with the deep almond richness of her hair, feel her "mountain flower" close to me beating, and all that. It was enough material for a thousand lifetimes. Maybe Eleanor was right: so much of Western thought had failed to access real truth because great men of ideas simply couldn't figure out how to get laid. This may be why philosophy, despite its namesake, largely steered clear of questions of love and sex, and when it did, approached it only in the drunken monologues of works like *The Symposium*, when Socrates' guard was down. And when Freud decided to take up the project of sex again, two-hundred centuries later, he could only talk about it in dirty terms, with Greek myths and genitalia. Failures, one after the other. Aristotle was awkward, Augustine hated sex, Schopenhauer hated women, Descartes was terrible in the sack, Kant was too preoccupied with purity, Kierkegaard was asexual, and Spinoza was too meek to ever slide up a stool.

I met Eleanor on the East Side, near the reservoir. It was getting cold in the late afternoon and she'd just finished a run. Steam rose from her skin. We walked along a stone wall stained with the shapes of old sunbaked magnolias, the kind that came alive in the city in the spring, in beautiful cream and pink, spreading their fragrance and dusting cars and bike seats with their pollen.

Eleanor wore a blue thermal jacket and black shorts that clung to her wet thighs. She'd started running in the evenings to spite her health issues. It was part of her ongoing dialogue with her body. Unlike me, she respected somatic calls for order. On her wrist was a smartwatch that recorded her steps, or heart rate, or pulse, or something. She waved me on, panting and sweat-glossed, as she pressed her fingers to the side of her windpipe.

The topic of this evening was our affair—mainly, the need for it to end, and whereas I was treating the matter with the upmost seriousness, Eleanor saw all of it in the oppressive glow of comedy. She saw our dalliance as a desperate act of two overeducated sad sacks, unable to govern their own lives.

"Why do you insist on making us both feel bad?" I said, as we followed the path surrounding the huge manmade lake with the black crowns of trees bared against the early evening.

"I'm just trying to remind you of what you already know—that we're both silly humans," she said. "We're both silly, and this is a desperate, silly little thing we're doing, isn't it?"

This talk troubled me. Nihilism had had a discreet edge over romance in our engagement. Eleanor was so ready to view our affair as a way of falling on a grenade, and it remained to be seen who was the grenade in this sacrificial gesture and who was doing the falling.

"I want us to be able to talk like rational humans, Eleanor. Can I speak plainly for a minute?"

"Surely you may."

"It's clear that we have the capacity to improve one another," I said. "Don't you feel it? This isn't just frivolity. We're exercising deep needs here, working through things. Why do you wish to trivialize this?"

"I don't accept that," she stopped, still breathless. "Do you know me to be the kind of person who trivializes things? I'm just trying to bring you down from your summit. You have such high notions about this little fling of ours."

"I won't deny it. But is that really so terrible?"

"Of course not. You know I love you, Paul. Atom for atom. But let's not be fools. What do you think's going to happen? I mean, what am I doing here?"

Whenever Eleanor said things like this, they had the weight of a loaded, existential question. I made desperate, weak-kneed appeals—claims about *Eros* being the best respite from *Thanatos*. I felt like a loveless diplomat, an ambassador from the Ministry of Lonely Hearts, here to broker a peace deal.

"I can't help you," she said. "I know what you want from me, and I can't give it to you."

"And what's that?"

"I can't be your muse, Paul. I've been there before. It's not a role I'm comfortable with. It doesn't suit me. Despite what you think."

She leaned on the back of a bench, still panting. She pulled the elastic through her wet hair and wrapped it around her wrist.

"What can I say about this, El?"

"You can say nothing."

She removed her jacket and wiped her face with the bottom of her shirt. Her body, along the contours of her stomach and back, had the curve and glare of dewy fruit.

"I just don't want there to be any resentment," I said.

"I stopped being resentful a long time ago. It costs too much. I used to really hate Jim for making a film out of me, but I've let that go. And things are better between us now."

"That's what he said. We had our talk. It was long coming."

"I know. He told me he gave you that cut above your ear."

She touched my left lobe with her wet hand, rubbing it the way you would a dog's.

"I wouldn't call him for a while," she said.

"We don't really talk anymore anyway. Ordinary conversation has deteriorated. We used to have these epic, six hours sessions, where we would speak without interruption. Like when Freud met Jung. But these days we can't go ten minutes without devolving into some petty dispute. The other day we argued about the pronunciation of *vehement*. I don't pronounce the H, see."

"You're just like an old couple. The two of you should get married."

We walked south toward the Great Lawn, in declining light. For distraction, I took to my surroundings, which also seemed to be resigning. The sky was in that blue and rose hour of the evening, the lamps still unlit and the baseball diamonds emptying. Behind a crowd of cherry blossoms and sycamore maples the Met looked like a fortress, deep and angular and dark.

"He gave me almost all the money he made from the film," she said. "It was his way of apologizing."

"How much is it?"

"In the millions. Not that it matters."

"What will you do?"

"I'm going to take a year or two off. Once my thesis is done. Maybe I'll travel the globe and get drunk with Karen in some third-world country. I like Karen."

"So do I."

Eleanor was looking at something on the other side of the path. She was adept at the oblique gaze, like so many city dwellers, a necessity of the enlisted voyeur, developed on subways and sidewalks. Then she looked directly at me, into me, seizing me with those blackpool eyes. In the waning light her cheeks were shadowed and ridged and through her thin mouth she smiled, flashing the gap that crenelated her two front teeth. I could tell she was sincere.

"I worry about you, Paul. You look like you haven't slept in a year. Aren't you done this thing of yours? Your great essay on the modern age?"

"America keeps me up, Eleanor. It prods me at all hours, day and night, informing me of its condition. The phrase 'don't lose sleep over it' should be taken literally now. And it astonishes me how people can ignore it. I don't know how van Winkle ever shut his eyes on this country."

We passed through the tented settlement, a colored suburb of leaning billowing polygons packed with heads and feet. Many carried on in a festive, fun-loving manner. Jean said the camps were about consciousness, and I'd once thought so as well, but I didn't see any consciousness in a single face sitting among us.

"You know, Jim owes me a considerable amount of money too," I said. "Maybe I'll emigrate for a bit, move to Europe and finance a year of self-examination. I'm long overdue for an expat phase."

"I don't think you're likely to get that now. I think he'll keep it as payment for you fucking me in secret for half a year."

We came across a group of college girls in alma mater sweaters, textbooks in their laps. Eleanor looked at them with mixed sympathy. They seemed newly hatched, still blind, with bits of shell in their hair.

"My tent's over here," she said. "Let's pack it up. I'm done with this."

We broke down her camp, wrapping up sleeping bags, collecting trash, packing her books into her bag. I picked up a folder containing her thesis and flipped through it, her great

Advance Reader Copy

criticism of love in the West. I remembered something Eleanor had once said about Jim and his film, how it was his way of using the right side of his brain to explain the left side of his life. She quoted a line from Valéry, a thing she'd taken to heart about what happened when the intellect forced itself on beauty: it installed theories in the place of feelings, replaced reality with an encyclopedia of memories; it transformed one's life into an endless library, making Venus into a document. She didn't exempt herself either. In a way, her thesis itself was a meta-criticism of this (you couldn't get out of explaining). She'd been in school for years trying to read her way into life so that she could live more closely with the things around her. And perhaps this explained her defection from the academy to the world of the encampments. For there was always too much reality and at the same time never enough of it. You either lived by *finesse*, as Pascal advised, and did with it what you could, or you rejected it altogether and played hooky with civilized life, as the people posting up here on the Great Lawn had chosen to do.

Then we found a patch of clean grass and watched the city's many nighttime lights assemble in their composite display, shifting, pairing off and forming long irregular rows. There was something of ritual in this act, like primitive man tracing idols between the stars, a pathology wondrous and deep and full of longing for the true contents of the heavens.

"You're in good humor again," Eleanor said as we exited the park. "Was it those girls back there? They were cute."

I laughed.

"See, you'll be okay," she said. "You fall in love with every girl and every building you see. You'll be fine as long as you have this city."

We parted sweetly. I went out the west entrance of the park and was in the street again. I cut in with the evening traffic, the sunlight falling through the buildings in clean shafts of bronze and the carousels spinning in doorways and people in suits coming languidly out into the air before disappearing into the mouths of subway stations; all of it buzzed in a pixel aura, a scattershot of occurrence, and I was content, for the moment, to let all of this be. There was another sign hanging from the neck of the Theodore Roosevelt statue, but I ignored it. I took the curb and headed north, and for a while I thought of nothing at all.

When I came home, I found Karen watching disaster footage on her computer. This time it was from a dam that had collapsed near a small riverine town somewhere in South America. It was the aftermath, the bright post-flow of rust-colored toxic sludge that had smashed its way through the jungle, staining the landscape and leaving villages buried in its wake. There were high wide aerial shots of riven earth, areas where the water carved new gullies and inlets; there was a fishing boat marooned in a red sea, razed hamlets, heaps of corrugated metal torn from mortar homes, downed telegraph wires, the dripping frames of upended vehicles, relief workers in orange suits, a copper faced kid with black eyes running up to the lens of the camera, his lashes clotted with riversilt.

A man spoke in babbling Portuguese.

The footage seemed to be arranged in chronological order, or rather, in a narrative sequence that felt the most like a story, with its progression of establishing shots and close-ups, so that you felt as if you were being taken through the full breadth of the experience. The final image showed mining waste blooming in the blue Atlantic, reaching and receding into layers of density before being called up and crested back onto the land in whitecapped waves.

The scenes rushed at you, wedged themselves into your headspace.

Karen flinched at a shot of a kid running up to the camera. It was a phantom presence, like the pang of a lost limb—she saw herself there with him, smelling him, his face in hers, keeping her arm out so he didn't crowd the frame.

Karen placed her palms together under her chin.

Nietzsche said that newspapers had replaced prayer in daily life. They were the new source of worldly reflection, when you contemplated the sufferings of others and the state of things elsewhere. The fleeting, ephemeral, transitory clutter of our lives had taken the place of the eternal, and it was the job of journalists like me and Karen, as the new priest class, to focus people and make sense of it. This required a certain derangement of the senses, as Baudelaire (that great documentarian of modern life) advised, a "frenzied journalism," which demanded that you be awake all the time. This may have been why Karen and I never seemed to sleep. But we needed to. We couldn't understand anything until we did. And now I felt like I could sleep for the next one hundred years. I was finally ready to close my eyes on the Republic.

They were showing shots of cows being airlifted out of mud. Feet down. Helpless in their harnesses. An old woman with a mud-stained face was wailing and shaking her hands at the heavens.

Karen blinked once.

She said she took photographs to locate herself. She gathered moments in little slips of memory and brought them across continents.

They showed people standing on a link of industrial pipe that ran alongside a mountain road, making visors of their hands and looking up at a shadowing helicopter.

Again the copper blooms and blue water.

Karen liked to say that images didn't pretend to explain anything. They didn't belong to an enterprise that had a special relationship to truth. They had no arrogance. They only teased at reality. They allowed you to extend your gaze and think: *if this is what it looks like, imagine how it must be.* And wherever she looked, she saw her work. The old divisions—home and abroad, the base and the field, the city and the county, private and public, here and there—didn't exist anymore. It didn't matter where you were. The field was everywhere and always. And now she was going back out again. Nothing could hide, after all. What is happening everywhere is known to us, one way or another.

This was Karen's project. She helped deliver the world, in her way, every day, bit by bit. She supplied the acquisitive spirit, opened up the nightmind, helped people imagine the full scope of the human experience, the so-muchness of life.

Document. Record. Disseminate. The world is the whole of the things we put into it.

Epilogue

That afternoon, I headed off toward the park. I felt the familiar downhill energy that one gets when traveling south through the island, watching the numbered streets run down slowly, block after block. I was happy to be outside in the late inclining sun and forgiving air, which was still in the preludes of a winter chill, with the avenues all in Christmas dress, wreaths on the lean black iron lamps and gold diode lights shaking on the trees lining the park wall. I was in need of rejuvenation. Since the publication of the essay, I hadn't written a word, and, while I wouldn't say I was depressed, I felt adrift, aimless in the absence of an organizing project around which to locate myself and carry me through my days.

In some respects, it didn't matter. These big, macrocosmic narratives could only account for so much of our lives. Even if you adhered your mind to an idea and lived by it devotedly, the world would still go about its indifferent business. During the fifties, for example, there were people who truly and wholeheartedly believed that the Eisenhower administration was in the pocket of the Kremlin, that the highest offices of the U.S. government had been infiltrated by communist agents— and if you happened to be the kind of person who believed this, you still had to pay your mortgage and buy groceries and drive your kids to school along with everybody else. Most of the time, even our deepest beliefs could only occupy about a tenth of our days (the essay elevated it to something like eighty percent, and now I'd been brought back down). The rest of the time, these ideas only laminated reality, offering objects an added glow, the aura that comes from the words and names that we give to things. In any case, I dismissed these questions and kept on. I knew I was in a mood and would soon get over this lowliness. An important event was taking place today, the last hurrah of the now defunct encampment, and all day I felt that something significant was going to occur, that whatever the Events were, whatever my theories about it had been, it was going to reveal itself in this last desperate grab for recognition.

The Great Lawn was emptying. By the time I got to 81st, people were already filing out into the streets. The mass headed down Central Park West, a stream of bodies hemmed in by saw horses. We spilled around the cars like water. The interplay of horns was deafening. These spontaneous demonstrations had been coordinated for this hour in all the major cities where camps still survived. It had been pretty much accepted that the whole thing had been a failure and this was a final outpouring of frustration and defeat.

I cut in with the throng and allowed myself to be carried forth as we flowed down toward the circle. Every few blocks crowds would break off and head to other destinations. I didn't partake in any of the chants and refused to carry the signs that were occasionally forced upon me. I was unable, as Jean suggested, to surrender myself to the mob mentality required for this kind of action.

Waves of sound rolled over the procession. Drum troupes. Chants. Megaphones. Sirens. The general thrum of ten-thousand bodies packed together. In the distance, the illumed white face of the Plaza Hotel rang above the tree line, its chateau design an old world reference that had been overruled by the soaring features of American business. I saw also the huge hideous rectilinear skyscraper that Jean and I had met in only a few weeks earlier, now its full height in the Midtown clutter, a long nondescript monolith rising through parallel geometry, one face in shadow, its windows spotted blue and orange.

The police were already out, in full riot gear, armor and shields, the lamps of their squad cars wagging blue and red. I saw people being snatched up, pressed to the ground, knees in their backs, thrown into cruisers. The demonstration had been planned for rush hour for the sake of maximum obstruction. But as we approached the roundabout at Columbus Circle there was another obstruction. The mass swirled around the wheel and broke off in two directions, down Broadway and 8th Ave., while another group formed around the circle's rostral column.

Over the bundled heads, the monument's fountains danced with plays of arcing, flying water, while on the outer edges people flooded through the belly of the giant shopping center. Many had stopped and were watching the scene through the grid of its curved glass facade. There were the dark twin edifices of the Time Warner building, reflected clouds rolling off on their mirrored fronts, and at whose base sat the sculpture of a huge globe made of polished steel, surrounded by a set of bright crossing rings resembling orbital paths.

We stopped. I couldn't see what was happening ahead, but I suspected that the police had responded quickly by setting up roadblocks on the streets, in order to prevent the demonstration from pouring down through the rest of the island. There was the sound of a horn, a galvanizing siren. People pressed at my back. In every direction it was nothing but clamoring bodies. A helicopter sounded overhead, dipping its glass nose low over the crowd and blowing off people's hats and sending signs in every direction. The mass began to push now, moving with heavy, desperate momentum. We were stepping on each other's feet. I lifted myself off the ground by placing my arms on the shoulders of the people next to me. I floated along for a bit and then tried to turn against the current. I pushed toward the south entrance of the park, heading for the gilded bronze monument of the USS Maine, the warrior women on her seashell chariot (resembling Venus), pulled by a troika of bright hippocampi. There were already some news crews in the crowd. I saw cameramen pinballing through the bodies, machinery on their shoulders. In the surrounding buildings I could see people gathered in the stacked glass windows, looking down on us. Almost all of them had their phones out, recording, streaming. I stopped for a moment, letting the crowd pass around me. I realized now that everyone—the whole world—was looking at us. The collective pressure was immense. We were all inside the event.

I heard shots. There was movement, a scattering. I was struck in the face, and then again, and then a third time, which blinded me and brought me to the ground. I fell to my knee, in darkness, my mouth sucking against the inside of my scarf. I covered my head and checked my nose briefly. As I moved to get up someone grabbed me and shoved me along. Shielding myself, I moved through a tantrum of haymakers. I caught another blow to the back of the head and fell against a perimeter railing. I saw canisters lobbed high over the crowd, trailing blue smoke in blooming colorful curls that struck and unfolded on the pavement. People pulled their shirts over their noses. Some were ready with bandanas. I wrapped my scarf around my face and held it there.

I saw police units now, appearing in the crowd, riot-ready. I inhaled the smell of gas. My eyes began to water. I could hear people gagging through their cupped hands. I scanned the linked barriers to find an exit. A young woman ran past me, branches of blood spilling down the side of her head. I stepped across discarded props, masks, and signs. There was a mass departure from the circle as people scrambled and hopped across the hoods of cars, horns all going off. They squeezed through exit barriers and hauled themselves over railings, some getting trapped underneath and trampled, while some fought back and screamed and were dragged to the ground. I watched two officers chase down a kid and lay their billies into his body, their polished black batons gleaming in fury. Magnesium flares arced overhead. Again the smoke cans, parabolic plumes of orange and blue.

Something drove itself into my chest. It was brief—a hot, glowing stiletto of pain. I fell down again, though I couldn't tell if I was hurt seriously. Crossing my arm, I held my hand to my left breast, near my armpit, keeping pressure on the spot. The police appeared as dark, armored figures through the haze.

People ran past me, milk streaming from their eyes. I felt my hand becoming wet. I lodged my index finger into my armpit and felt something hard and searing in the fleshy pocket like razor metal, shredded and pulpy. It was a modest wound. I saw colored smoke and the smeared yellow shapes of taxis and the vertical jigsaw-like light of surrounding buildings. Everything became fluid, bleeding and radiant.

I escaped the circle and cut across the plaza, liquefactions of things spilling past. Black storm-trooping units ran around me, recognizing I wasn't a threat. I stumbled into the lobby of a nearby hotel. The heavy doors swung open and the air vents carried me into a bright interior of steel and glass. I heard Christmas music. Some hotel attendants rushed toward me and tried to move me along. I waved them away and said I was fine. I followed a spiral stair, taking the steps slowly. Beneath my jacket, I felt my shirt soaking up with blood. At the top of the stair was a lounge with a view of the circle. People were gathered along the window, looking down. I decided to stay. I ordered a beer and sat in a booth next to the glass. Despite being in serious pain, I felt remarkably lucid. It was a heightened awareness, like I'd just been through a car crash—a feeling super-real.

The televisions mounted above the bar were turned to the news. All the stations had split screens—on one side, anchors gathered around their desks in bright studios at the top of these very Midtown buildings, graphic skylines in their backgrounds; and on the other, live footage of the scenes playing out in the streets below. The hosts were commenting, analyzing, leaning over their desks, trying their best to improvise some insight and give people a sense of immediate perspective. I heard them saying things like, "I think ultimately what we're seeing here is…" or, "There is no doubt that this will be a pivotal…" There was footage of crowds in the lower districts of Manhattan, gathered outside the stock exchange, hurling objects at its classical façade, cellphone footage of people storming the subways, offices and lobbies being ransacked as people made their way up into buildings. There was also footage from other camps, in Baltimore, Philadelphia, Atlanta and D.C., where the demonstrators had been stopped on their march toward the Capitol Building.

Despite this, everything seemed remarkably calm around me. Everyone was still hushed at the window. I looked down and saw riot police dispersing people up and down Central Park West, forming a perimeter and blocking off the circle, then I looked up and saw the exact same scene on the screens above the bar, from nearly the same vantage, as if the camera was placed exactly where I was sitting at this moment. It seemed, almost, like it was my own vision that was being broadcast.

I sat there for a time in silence. I don't know how long. Drinking my beer. I got a text. It was from Eleanor. It said: "Are you seeing this?" I ignored it. Then I got another text, this time from Karen. It said the same thing. Then my phone started exploding with messages. I turned it over and leaned my head against the window, which was cold and nice against my cheek.

After a few minutes a young girl came over and sat across from me. She was a student, by the look of it—collegiate sweater, short chestnut hair, glasses with thick black frames. She reminded me a bit of Eleanor.

"What happened?" she said.

I said I didn't know. I squinted.

"Did you see it?" she said. "Were you there?"

"Yes," I said. "I was there."

Then she held up her phone. On the screen was my essay, or what I thought was my essay. The light glared on its glass face.

"I read this this morning," she said.

"That's nice, thank you."

"I have some thoughts. Can I email you about it?"

"Certainly," I said. "I'd like that."

By the time I made it back outside, an hour or so later, the circle was empty. There was debris scattered everywhere. I saw bloodstains on the asphalt, people's gloves, bags, rocks, signs, smoke canisters. A few people were drifting about, crying, not knowing where to go. The police were still out, holding their perimeter. The air was mild, pleasant. My vision adjusted to the darkness. A nice night, I thought. The subway entrances around the circle were blocked off. I walked north, along the park. I could tell that most of my shirt was soaked now, and it sucked against my stomach. The people around me seemed unconcerned. Did they know what had just occurred? What they'd just been a part of? Were they a part of anything at all?

This wound would need to be treated. But I could do that later. It wasn't bad. I stuck my finger in my jacket and traced the shredded hole with my finger and suddenly felt an affection for it. The subway rumbled under the street and I received its vibrations through the soles of my shoes. I knelt down and touched a patch of grass, feeling the hum beneath me.

I trudged back home, limping through the streets. I must have looked like Belmondo at the end of *Breathless*, staggering dramatically down the avenue. When I returned, my building was quiet. Everyone was in their rooms. I walked down the hallway and heard the sound of different programs running behind doors. My apartment was dark. On the table was a bottle of alcohol Karen had left me as a gift, along with some contact information and a list of places she would be in the coming weeks.

I opened the tap and let the bath fill up. Then I sat down at my desk. The computer awoke from its sleep, showing the news page I'd left open. I refreshed it. All the breaking stories, of course, were about what had just happened. Down the page there was some other stuff, some EU trade negotiations and a story about a bunch of people getting sick in some northern Chinese city. I closed it. Behind, waiting on my desktop, was a blank document in the center of the screen, gaping, waiting to have its white space filled up. I closed it as well.

I was still coming down from the publication of the essay. It proved to be a major success. Everyone had been talking about it, applauding it, affirming it. I'd been getting calls all week and my following online had doubled in just a few days. Not only was it successful, it was also one hundred percent true and correct in its insight—and its trueness had been acknowledged. But true as it was, I'd walked outside that afternoon and everything had looked the same; nothing had changed by me sending my thoughts out into the world. There was that peculiar German belief that you could reconcile the universe with your consciousness and make it answer to your perception. But to believe this, you had to believe that the universe graduated along with you, entering into higher categories of awareness as you progressed through these stages of knowledge—as if the universe cared about your thoughts!

Not only would the world not stop, it was going to push on, quickly and indifferently, and in a week, everyone would forget about what I'd said. As true and good and right as my essay was, the events of today were about to replace it in people's minds. Now everything was about the demonstrations. Jean had gotten his wish, his putsch on human attention. But soon enough this too would be over. Like my essay, it would get absorbed, swallowed up into the culture's great perpetual motion machine, which had an endless capacity for assimilation, far exceeding any individual's. The essay had been my attempt to try to establish a narrative, yes—a way of explaining things. I thought that if I could just explain the culture to itself that it would understand and then act accordingly. But this didn't happen. And anyway, how could this effort compete with the culture itself, which was writing its own grand narrative a million times a minute, every moment of every day, sucking up and integrating all other narratives into it? How did you compete with this? Your only hope was to join the stream, to get sucked in too and allow yourself to be carried along with it.

Riffling off these thoughts gave me some assurance. I was still thinking straight. I wasn't delirious, or dying. I would have to get this wound treated. Later though. At the moment, all I wanted to do was lie in the tub for a bit. I slid into my usual position, not bothering to take my clothes off. The wound seared. It wasn't too bad; it was mostly flesh and muscle and too close to the shoulder to be near any vital organs or arteries, nothing that could cause serious damage. I wanted to sit with it for a while and enjoy the clarity it gave me. Warm threads of blood curled out into the water, delicately, gracefully. I draped my arm over the rim. It was nice. Someone should be here to depict this, I thought.

I realized my phone was still in my pocket. I took it out and held it underwater. The screen flashed. The throbber lit up in its clockwise circuit, did a few laps and then went dead.

Before me now was the south sky, a glimmering cipher of light, a thousand radiating pixels that streamed into my vision, crawling up my synapses and settling somewhere there, becoming little realities. I heard voices in the streets, horns, the sighing breeze in the trees. The ruins of the evening were settling back into something familiar. A plane rolled low overhead, its wing lights flashing against a dark band of clouds. I thought of the people seated in the sky, shuttling across the lonely latitudes of the globe, and I thought of Bill, or rather Bill's remains, hurtling somewhere above the atmosphere at their escape velocity, slingshotting around me. And I thought of all the words and ideas that we erect in the interstices, the cities that we make in abstract space. It all fights for recognition. And what do we do with all this consciousness? I decided to leave the question alone for a while.

Everything was calm. I could feel the moment receding, things beginning to ebb. But even now, barely coming down from this latest crisis, it seemed as if we were already approaching another, a great wave, various and terrible and new, massed with disastrous *potentia*, one that would command the attention of us all. Then a quote arose in my mind, unannounced, as if out of the ether, a line by somebody, I couldn't recall whom, about owls and twilight, about using grey to paint grey, or something to that effect. I wasn't able to remember. Anyway, it didn't seem to matter much now. I had nothing more to say.